PENGUIN BOOKS

# KISSES IN THE NEDERENDS

Epeli Hau'ofa was born in Papua New Guinea in 1939 to Tongan missionary parents. He went to school in Papua New Guinea, Tonga, Fiji and Australia, and attended the University of New England, Armidale, NSW; McGill University, Montreal; and the Australian National University, Canberra, where he gained a PhD in social anthropology. He taught briefly at the University of Papua New Guinea, and was a research fellow at the University of the South Pacific in Suva, Fiji. From 1978 to 1981 he was Deputy Private Secretary to His Majesty the King of Tonga, and in early 1981 he re-joined the University of the South Pacific as the first director of the newly created Rural Development Centre based in Tonga. Since 1983 he has been Head of the Department of Sociology at the University.

Epeli Hau'ofa is author of *Tales of the Tikongs*, a collection of short stories, and three works of non-fiction: *Mekeo*, *Corned Beef and Tapioca* and *Our Crowded Islands*. He lives in Suva with his long-suffering wife Barbara, stroppy son Epeli junior, aged ten and, he says, growing up too fast for anyone's good, and two de-sexed pets, Gipsy and Patch, who pay him no respect whatever.

82 rte

Marama's working hours were divided into two periods, before and after lunch. The morning sessions were for the really sick and diseased; afternoons – which often extended well into evening – were largely for the information-exchange service. She was thoroughly disliked but, as she put it, had almost everyone by the balls.

The Health Centre nurse, one of Marama's main sources of information, had sneaked out as soon as Dr Tauvi Mate had finished examining Oilei. She went straight to Marama's and whispered something in her ear. Marama quickly adjourned the afternoon session and waddled over to Oilei's house. Mere and Makarita were already there; although they disliked her heartily, they could not send her away. She already had them by the balls too.

Five minutes later Oilei staggered into the house. He was furious at finding Marama there because he realised then that the news of his misfortune had already been broadcast throughout the village, and would very soon spread beyond to other communities. He now hoped that no one apart from his wife and mother-in-law knew what his real problem was. Everyone in the village would know only that Makarita had splashed hot water over him.

Of course people would talk about it for two or three days but they would soon move on to other things. Korodamu had the reputation for producing major scandals at the rate of two a week; minor ones happened every minute.

After his initial shock at finding Marama sitting in his living room, Oilei put on the best possible face, greeted her and sat down heavily on a solid chair. He muffled a cry of agony, went down on all fours and stretched himself out on the floor, moaning.

'So, it's something else, isn't it?' Marama asked.

'What do you mean?' Alarm bells rang with every word.

'And it doesn't look like tummy ache either.'

'It's the scalding I got.'

'Really, Oilei. Who do you take me for? You should be much more careful talking to me. I've seen dozens of cases exactly like yours. Anyway, I'm here to help you.'

'I don't need your help. If I want help I'll go to the hospital. I hate bush medicine.'

'I know you well enough, Oilei Bomboki, to tell you that you're not going near any hospital. What, and let all those loose-tongued nurses look up your orifice?'

'Who says I've got pain in the arse? Oh, shit!'

'Really. Did I say anything about anyone's arse? But now that you've mentioned your own, perhaps that's where the problem is. You've made me jump the gun. We must always do things properly and begin from the end.' Marama rummaged through her handbag, pulled out a small roll of leaves, a piece of ginger and three whole chillies. She ate the leaves with the chillies, munching them with her few remaining teeth. She chewed slowly and carefully swallowed everything before she took the ginger.

Everyone was quiet. Marama closed her eyes, stretched herself out on the floor and was soon sound asleep. She snored exactly like Makarita, except that her tongue hung out and her whole body shook as she breathed. Then out of the blue she fired the first volley of farts that swept the room with the rat-a-tat of a machine gun. A brief lull was shattered by a convoy of army trucks cruising at a hundred miles an hour. All the while Marama's body jerked convulsively without waking her. The whole room stank. Mere and Makarita covered their faces with handkerchiefs, doing their best not to burst out laughing, while on the floor Oilei groaned and giggled at the same time. Then, as suddenly as it started, the performance ceased and in a little while Marama opened her eyes slowly, sat up, rearranged her clothes and wiped her face.

'Tell me, Rita, what did I do while asleep?'

'You snored and . . .' Rita bit her hand trying to maintain a semblance of dignity.

'You shouldn't do that. This is very serious. Now, Oilei, what else did I do?'

'I didn't see anyone do anything. But I think I heard a replay of the Battle of the Bulge. And the whole place stank like a shithouse, I beg your pardon . . .'

'No need to apologise. Now, listen carefully, both of you. Your different perceptions of what happened are very important. A few minutes ago I slept as two persons; as you, and you,' she pointed to each in turn. 'In my line of work I can become any number of people all at once. You noticed that I snored and farted simultaneously, and that neither interrupted the other. Now, partly because of your different answers to my questions, I can tell you this, and it's absolutely accurate.' She gave Makarita a narrow-eyed look. 'You're an incurable snorer.'

Rita was taken aback but Marama had shifted her attention to Oilei. 'You fart too much. That's why you've got pain in the arse. But it's all because of Rita . . .'

'I knew it! I knew she was responsible, the silly bitch. Oh, shit!'

'Don't blame me. Blame your own arsehole!'

'Stop this nonsense at once!' Marama cut in sternly. 'I'm not here to watch domestic scenes. Do it when I'm gone, although I advise you to start acting your age. I'm here only because I'm interested in solving Oilei's problem.' She paused to let the air cool down.

'You see, farting has many and varied causes,' Marama resumed, speaking in the tone of a lecturer addressing a group of new students. 'At any point of time there are many varieties of fart, each and every one of which is rooted in the history of our people. There are clean farts and there are dirty farts; farts that drown out thunders and farts quieter than silence; there are good farts that angels make and evil farts that come out of Satan's blowhole. But the worst type is called "double-fart", caused by breathing other people's snores. Snoring is the expulsion of fart through the mouth; that's why it's so noisy. When your body is saturated with farting gases, most of them come out through the upper orifice, the lower one being too small to handle it all. The inhalation of fart from a snorer's mouth is no different from breathing fart that comes out of the other end. What Oilei did to you this morning, Rita, was no different from what you've been dishing out to him for many years. And that's what caused his problem, as you will see. If you breathe in second-hand fart, it gets mixed up with your original product and the result is known as a double-fart. Students at the university call it the "lecturer fart", for reasons known only to

11

themselves. We shall call it that because it sounds intellectual. By the way, the mucus in the nose and throat, which is said to be caused by cold, is really condensed fart. It looks exactly like condensed milk, which is liquefied cow fart.

'Lecturer fart can lead to many problems. It can collect in the stomach and distend it. Anyone with a big tummy is full of fart, not shit as is commonly believed. That's why only fat people are called windbags. Lecturer fart can seep into the scrotum socket and blow it up to the size of a soccer ball. That's what most of our important people have. VIPs sit around and do no physical work, not because of their eminence as is generally assumed, but because they carry enormous soccer balls, which make them unable to walk properly. They sit on chairs behind huge desks to hide their balloons. That's why they're so cranky and bossy.

'Lecturer fart can also collect in the arse and solidify into tiny little stones that cling like limpets to the anal wall. Sometimes these stones loosen their grip and roll around inside the arse, causing tremendous agony like what you have, Oilei. They never roll out on their own volition. If you put your finger inside and try to get at them, they merely roll up and out of reach. Often these stones would roll too high up to find their way back easily. Most of them would eventually return to their proper places, but every so often a few would really get lost and lodge themselves in the kidney and the gall bladder, where the environments are very hospitable. There they are mistakenly called kidney and gall stones by ignorant doctors. They're very difficult to get rid of. I just heard from a science professor at the university that the Chinese have gone so far as to blast them into smithereens with tiny nuclear bombs. We don't have to go to that extreme in our treatment, thank God.

'Oilei, your arse's in a real mess. There are probably four hundred fart stones rolling around inside. We must get rid of them, but first things first. You and Makarita must not sleep in the same room again. In fact, snorers should be isolated from the rest of humanity. Makarita, from now on you sleep in one of the spare bedrooms, where you can snore to your heart's content and hurt no one.

12

'The next step is for me to give you medicine to rid yourself of your problem. There will be two types of medicine. You take the first one tonight and the other tomorrow morning. You must take the right medicine first or you will have a bigger problem and may even develop a soccer ball. The first lot will cleanse your system of any trace of the lecturer fart. The other lot will enable you to fart out all the stones from your arse. You won't feel anything except extreme tiredness through losing too much air. But in the end your arse will come out smooth as a baby's bottom. And Makarita, get your recorder and tape whatever happens. I want to hear it later. I must go now. Someone will come with the medicine.'

Just before sundown a pair of small, smelly boys, grinning from ear to ear, arrived with two rolls of leaves with ginger and chillies inside. They presented the medicine meekly to Makarita and peeked around her into the room where Oilei was still on the floor moaning. Makarita grabbed them firmly by the ear and marched them out to the street. As soon as she released them they shot off, loudly imitating Oilei's moans.

Makarita stormed furiously back into the house and towered over her prostrate husband. 'Look at what you've done! You've shamed us all! Everyone here knows what you've got. They're all laughing. Dear Lord, why did you make me marry him?'

Oilei was not in a condition to say anything. He just lay there helplessly moaning and groaning, a fallen giant. He looked so pathetic that Makarita was touched. She sat down by him and took his head onto her lap whispering, 'I'm so sorry. Forgive me. I'm sorry.' They remained like this for a while until Makarita remembered the medicine. She gave him a roll of leaves, which he chewed painfully and had much difficulty in swallowing. As soon as he finished he fell asleep. He was so still that Makarita checked his pulse and gave a sigh of relief. She let his head down on a cushion and went and got the tape deck ready.

Then it started; everything went off simultaneously. Makarita switched on the tape and opened all the windows. Oilei snored and farted simultaneously. It was thunder, motorbike, machine guns and kettledrums blasting away.

13

'Dear Lord, please don't let him burst. Look! Mere, look! He's going to burst open!'

But Oilei did not; he merely bloated with gas then slowly subsided to normality as he fired away. His explosions tossed and bounced him around like a deflating balloon. Makarita pounced and held him down by the shoulders. Mere grabbed for his legs but was thrown back by a tremendous boom, which began the expulsion of the lecturer fart that soon filled the lounge. Both women rushed outside gasping for fresh air; Caesar streaked inside and out again as fast as his legs could move. All this lasted about ten minutes, by which time most of the lecturer fart had been expelled except for tiny pockets that remained trapped here and there. Oilei began breathing easily from both ends. The good fart had begun to take over. Every so often he would loudly blast out a mediocre pocket of the lecturer fart, and by midnight there was complete peace. Makarita switched off the recorder and went to bed.

Next morning Oilei opened his eyes at about six. He felt absolutely weak but still had enough wit about him to feel the pain. His moans brought Makarita into the lounge, where he had spent the night. She gave him the other roll of leaves, which he duly chewed and swallowed with even greater difficulty than before. Soon after, he rolled over and passed out.

What Makarita saw and heard there and then were to remain indelibly etched in her brain for the rest of her life. Trumpets blew, trombones blared, violins strained and kettledrums rumbled. The house shook; but as suddenly as it came the cacophony went, only to be replaced by the thirty-six-inch guns of the USS *Navarone* pounding the shores of Vietnam. Then, to Makarita's horror, Oilei levitated.

'Mere! Mere! he's floating away! Sweet Mother of God, please don't take him away yet!' Makarita pounced once again, pressed him down to the floor and threw herself across his middle. Having learnt from her earlier mistake, Mere sat on Oilei's head only to be hit full in the tail by a tremendous snore. She jumped off and screamed, 'Eeeee! The fuckwit farted into my arse! Oh! Oh!' All the while Oilei stayed fast asleep, blasting away from both ends.

Twenty minutes later, when there was a lull, Makarita stuck her hand through the top of Oilei's pyjama pants, feeling for the stones that had been blown out. There was none. She checked again, and looked into his mouth and the area around his head. Nothing there. And for the rest of the day Oilei farted occasionally without dislodging a single stone. Although it was all over by sunset, he did not once open his eyes. Makarita took turns with Mere to keep vigil over him through the night.

When he woke up the following morning Oilei was drained of all energy and could only manage a feeble whine to indicate that the pain had not abated.

'There's something terribly wrong,' Mere concluded. 'Go to Marama for further instructions. Hurry up, Rita.'

Makarita was conscious of eyes following her every step and of tongues wagging behind half-closed doors. She could hear barely suppressed sniggers and feel people poking each other's ribs, pointing at her. She sensed all this even before she had stepped out of her house. She was furious with her mother for sending her. Mere should have gone herself, being older and more inured to village talk. She was also a formidable tongue-lasher, with whom village women were careful when talking. But Makarita knew that it was her responsibility to see Marama, not Mere's.

She pulled herself together and stepped out carrying the tape recorder and several cassettes. If anyone dares try anything on me, I'll tear their eyes out, she kept telling herself. As she walked by the first house a voice sang out, 'Morning, Rita. How are you?' It was Vani, the head Sunday-school teacher.

'So so. And you?'

'So so. Where've you been?'

What a stupid question, Makarita thought to herself, she knows damn well I've just left home. 'From there,' she gave the usual reply.

'And where're you going?'

'Over there,' Makarita replied, pointing her index finger at a direction roughly a quarter-way up into the sky.

'What for?'

Although such questions were merely form and people did not normally expect any real answers, Makarita was alertly suspicious because of what had just happened. None of your bloody business, she muttered inaudibly, but aloud, 'Oh, I'm just going to do something. What are you doing?'

'Just this. How's Oilei?'

Watch this carefully. 'So so. And how's Tevita?' O God, you've done it; she nearly bit her tongue for not controlling itself better.

'He's a bit so so. In bed with a little pain the last time I saw him, heh, heh.'

'Oh. That's a pity.' This time she really bit her tongue. It should never have responded.

'Yes. Just a slight pain on his thigh. But some people are more fortunate than others. He'll be up and jumping within six months if he's lucky. The pain's spreading upward though. I've heard of people who've got it right up their you know what. I hope Oilei's so so's not too so so. Bye.'

'Yeah, bye.' I'll get you one of these days, you scurvy bitch. Makarita increased her speed.

'Hello, Rita. How're you?' It was Komo, the biggest teaser in the district, sitting on her verandah weaving a mat.

'So so, thanks. And you?'

'So so. I'm not so sure, you know.'

'Yes, maybe.'

'Are you going there?'

'Where?' Makarita was taken aback.

'There,' Komo replied, indicating with her head the general direction where Makarita was going.

'Oh. Yes, that way and the other, you know.'

'Yes, maybe. Where's Oilei?'

'Over there. Where's Jone?'

'Are you there, Jone?' Komo called out aloud. No response. 'Jone, are you there?'

'No! I'm not there!' came a booming reply from somewhere at the back.

'He's not there,' she told Makarita. 'Where are you then?'

'In here!'

'He's in here,' she told Makarita.

16

'Where?' she called out again, louder than before.

'In the bloody loo, you silly bitch!'

'He's in the toilet. Been cranky since he woke up.'

'I wonder why,' Makarita said with a smirk.

'What're you doing there?' Komo called out again.

'Posting a parcel to your stupid father, for Chrissake! Do you want the whole bloody world to know?'

'They can't hear you! Why don't you post it in small lots? Much easier that way, you know.'

'Belt up, you stinking old fart! You're interrupting.'

'We're interrupting,' Komo said.

'Where's the toilet paper?' Jone called.

'In there.'

'Where?'

'Look around.'

'There's nothing here. Get me one, will you.'

'I'm busy. Wait till I'm finished.'

'For Chrissake, get some bloody paper!'

'Get it yourself.'

'How could I, you stupid old hag!'

'Don't swear at me, everyone might hear! I'd use my left hand if I were you!'

'I'll kill you!'

'Why not right now?' Komo looked at Makarita. 'He's a pain in the arse. Is Oilei a pain in the arse?' she asked with a glint in her eyes.

'Well, er, see you later. Bye.'

'Mmmmm.'

I'll shred you one day, I will, Makarita raged under her breath as she moved on.

'Hey, good morning, Rita. How're you?' It was Amelia, living two houses down from Komo's. A great gossip, Amelia was.

'Morning, Lia. I'm so so. And you?'

'So so. Where're you off to so early?'

'Over there to do something. What're you doing?'

'Nothing really. I'm just doing this before I do that. How's Oilei? Heard he'd had an accident or something.'

'Oh, it's something very minor. He'll be right pretty soon.'

17

'Let's hope so. But we must always take care of minor things mustn't we? They could easily develop into major pains in the neck, you know. I was saying to Miri just the other day . . . talk of the devil! Hello, Miri. Looking tiptop this morning you are. Must've eaten a banana for breakfast or something.'

'Better than your hotdog lunch, thank you for shutting up. Well, well, Rita! How're you? Sorry about Oilei. How's he coming along? Heard he's got such headache he couldn't breathe properly. Too much gas in the brain, you know what I mean. If he's not careful it'll spread down. But don't worry, Rita. I've got this potion just for that kind of thing. I'm taking it to him . . . But what about you? Where're you off to?'

'Over there. You go ahead. Mere's with him. I'll be there soon. Bye.' She resumed her journey. She wanted to run but that would only attract more attention and even running commentary. I wish I were invisible, she mumbled to herself and nearly ran smack into Filo.

'Rita! So good to see you! You look bushed. Are you OK?'

Shit! Not another one heading home. 'I'm so so, Filo. Nothing to concern anyone. Where're you going?'

'Over there . . . I mean, to your place. Tell you what,' she said conspiratorially, 'he'll be up and kicking soon as he's taken his special something. He takes it once and he'll be jumping around. Just like those Germans last year. Haven't you heard that whites have been coming home for my medicine? Fixed them right there and then. No problem. You looking for something?'

'No, not really. I'm taking a little walk, that's all. I need some fresh air. Stayed up all night, you know.'

'You should be in bed then. You're not sleepwalking, are you?'

'Oh, no. I'm too tired to sleep. Go ahead, I'll be back soon.' Spare me, Lord. The next one I meet will go minus her tongue. She jumped at the gentle tap on shoulder. 'What the fucking . . . Oh, I'm terribly sorry, Pastor. You surprised me so.'

'Dear oh dear. We must never say "fuck",' said the Reverend Masu Lasu. 'I understand your situation. You must be under tremendous stress. But have faith and Oilei will recover soon. Don't put your trust in man-made medicines. Only the Lord can

18

heal the afflicted. You should have more faith in the Lord than you have shown. I must go to Oilei. I expect to see you later.'

Struck dumb by what she had said, Makarita merely nodded and moved on. To her enormous relief there were no visitors at Marama's; it was still too early and the old lady was inside playing with her great-grandchildren, who melted away as they had been trained as soon as Makarita entered.

'It's bad news, isn't it?'

'Yes, it is,' Makarita replied tearfully.

'Let's hear it then.'

Makarita described in detail what had happened and how at the end of it all not one stone had been blown out. Marama considered this and told Makarita to play the tapes while she listened quietly, nodding her head here and shaking it there, her eyes tightly closed. Halfway through the first side of the first tape she indicated to Makarita to stop.

'That's enough. I know the problem. How well did he chew the leaves?'

'As I told you, he was so weak he couldn't do it properly. He could only just swallow the stuff.'

'Yes. That came out clearly from the tape. I don't mean the chewing and swallowing, but their effect on his performance. Had he chewed the medicine well he would have released its full power. As it was, there wasn't enough power to even blow out all the lecturer fart. That's why no stone came out.'

'But he farted so much. You heard it . . .'

'That was only half strength. Nowhere near what it should have been. Believe me, I know what I'm talking about. You should have seen that New Zealander who took it last year. His wife had a mild heart attack just watching him perform. But he shot out three hundred, all within an hour.'

'What can we do, then?'

'There's no question of him taking another dose of the medicine or any other. It'll blow him to bits if he takes it again within six months.'

'But you said it was only half strength . . .'

'Don't tempt fate, Rita. Half strength of my medicine's many times stronger than any other in Tipota. No one has taken it

19

more than twice. As I said, he shouldn't take any other medicine through the mouth. His body's too weak to tolerate anything; you've seen it yourself. We must try something else. Let me think for a little while.' For about half a minute Marama racked her photographic memory until she found what she wanted.

'We must get Losana Tonoka. She's what Oilei needs at this stage. A faith-healer. No medicine. She prays, lays her hands on stricken organs and the patient's off and running. She runs rings around Oral Roberts's imitators, hopeless quacks they are. Oilei will be in good hands. Lo has healed many Peace Corps volunteers, you know. I'm off to Kuruti for a four-day conference. Lo will be there. I'll bring her here afterwards. In the meantime, go home and look after your husband. Remember not to let him take any medicine.'

Makarita thanked Marama profusely, slipped a sealed envelope on the floor in front of her and left. When Marama found that it contained two two-dollar bills she was pleased, for she rarely received any money from her clients, most of whom were poor.

Even the well-off offered her only food, which made her fat but still penniless. It did not worry her, for she had renown and power verging on the mystical.

On reaching home Makarita was struck by the silence inside, punctuated only by Oielei's moans from the bedroom, where he had taken himself when visitors started arriving. Miri, Filo, Rev. Masu Lasu and Mere were quietly sipping tea, waiting for Makarita to return.

'Mere, has Oilei taken any medicine since I left?' Makarita asked anxiously.

'He refused to touch anything,' Mere replied indignantly. 'Filo and Miri tried to get him to but he told them to stick it up their jumpers. Very rude and abusive he is. Deserves whatever he's got, I say.'

'Thank heavens for that. Just make sure he doesn't take any medicine.'

'Look, Rita, mine's a very good brew,' Filo protested. 'He only has to take it once and he'll be singing right away instead of groaning.'

20

'Sorry, but that's my instruction from Marama,' Makarita countered, without feeling sorry.

'What does that baggy old hag know about my medicine?'

'Do you want to say that to her face or shall I do it for you?'

'I was only trying to be helpful,' Filo piped back weakly. She had no stomach for any kind of confrontation with Marama.

'We shouldn't bicker while there's suffering in the house,' the pastor intervened. 'We're here to help Oilei. There's no better medicine on earth than faith in the Lord. Let's go in and lead him to the healing arms of Jesus.' Rev. Masu Lasu rose, took his chair and led the way into the bedroom. The others followed suit and knelt around the bed. Masu Lasu sat on the chair beside Oilei's head, which he touched gently.

'That's not where it's at, dummy. It's way down the other end. Oh, shit!'

Rev. Masu Lasu ignored the remark. 'In the name of the Father, Son and the Holy Ghost, amen,' he intoned ecumenically, straightened up and continued, 'Mere, Rita and our sisters in the Lord. We're here to witness the marvellous, mysterious doings of our Saviour. It's obvious that the Almighty is testing brother Oilei as he tested that great Israelite, Job of the Old Testament. As you know, Job was a wealthy man whose piety was known to all. Likewise, brother Oilei is a wealthy man whose piety is virtually non-existent.

'When the Lord saw Job's wealth and piety, he told his angels, "Go and test his faith." The angels flew down and destroyed Job's wealth: his cattle, goats, sheep, and chickens, and burnt down his barns and houses. They also killed his many wives and children, everyone that he dearly loved.'

'They should've started with Rita and Mere. Oh, shit!'

'You can't annoy us with your blasphemy, Brother Oilei. You're no longer responsible for your behaviour,' Rev. Masu Lasu retorted without ire. 'In view of the calamity befallen him, did Job lose faith in the Lord? Not one bit. His bereavement served only to strengthen his faith. On seeing this, the Lord was pleased but told his angels to put Job through further trials and get the full measure of his devotion. The angels went down and inflicted upon him all kinds of diseases: leprosy, beriberi, ulcer, headache, gout, elephantiasis, diabetes, scurvy, ringworm and to top it all they covered Job with boils from head to toe. Which of course included the kind of boils Brother Oilei suffers from.'

'Bullshit! I've got no fucking boils. It's stones in the arse, like stones in the kidney. Oh, shit!'

'Job had stones in the arsehole too, Brother Oilei. He did. But he neither complained, nor groaned, nor made song and dance about it . . .'

'Who's singing and dancing with a pain in the arse, for Chrissake!'

'Mind your language, Brother Oilei. It's extremely blasphemous. There are in this room ladies with clean souls and sensitive ears.'

'Mere with sensitive ears? And Rita with a clean soul? You don't know a bloody thing, Pastor.'

'You must take hold of yourself, Brother Oilei.'

'Hold your own self and shake it too, heh, heh. Oh, shit!'

'Ladies, please ignore his crude remarks. Brother Oilei's under such pain he can't control himself. Now, let's return to Job. Despite all that he suffered, Job's faith strengthened tenfold, which so impressed the Lord that he told his angels to remove his afflictions and give him his just rewards. The angels went down, restored Job's health and gave him ten times more wealth, wives and children than he had before. And he lived happily for the rest of his earthly life.

'Brother Oilei, the Lord's testing you. It's only the beginning. Tougher trials, which will shake the very foundation of your faith, are yet to come.'

'Bullshit! This is no fucking test. It's torture!' And Oilei suddenly doubled up as a jab of pain struck his arse and shook him from head to toe.

'The Lord giveth and the Lord taketh. He has given you pain and only he can take it away . . .'

'Take your arse out of my house, and don't bring it back here again. Oh, shit!'

'Very well, Brother Oilei. But let me leave this with you. Everything from now on will depend on the strength of your faith. You must have it in order to endure what's coming without

22

flinching. It will get progressively worse and may even lead to your early and unexpected departure from your corrupt mortality. But eternal happiness awaits the true believer. Goodbye and God bless you. I may or may not see you again in this life. But I'll be back this evening and if you're still with us, God willing, we shall sing his praise.'

'Drop dead!' Oilei's parting shot followed the pastor out of the room.

It was the last the pastor saw of Oilei, and vice versa. That very afternoon the angels of the Lord put the Reverend Masu Lasu through so severe a test that his heart stopped beating altogether.

2

Losana Tonoka was the spinster elder sister of the ratai, chief of Tumunu, largest of the three clans of Thangilamba, a village on the south-eastern tip of Tipota and sixty kilometres from Korodamu. Losana's great-great-grandfather, Ratai Tevoro Levu, was the last of the heathen chiefs to hold out against the marauding forces of Christianity. He had fought valiantly and ferociously but in the end he had to surrender to the superior forces of the foreign god. He promptly accepted the new religion in order to save his followers' lives, but his conversion was nominal: to the end of his life he adamantly refused to be baptised, attend church services, contribute anything whatever to church activities, or learn how to read and write.

During the upheaval, Ratai Tevoro took under his protection the heathen gods that had been expelled by their erstwhile worshippers when they converted to the foreigners' religion. He sent his followers surreptitiously to collect stone and wooden images of the discarded ancient gods, which he stored in underground vaults he had built on his land. Since that time the ratai of Tumunu's land and everything grown, living or stored on it had been protected effectively by the grateful old deities. Although Tipotans had been Christians for over a century, they had not shed their fear of spirits. The new religion merely downgraded their native gods to the rank of malicious ghosts, who roamed everywhere and did horrible things to people. The Holy Ghost might reign in heaven, but Tipota was the happy hunting ground for the lesser spirits.

The lineage of the ratai of Tumunu had always been the foremost faith-healing family in the country. This premier position was secured for all time when Ratai Tevoro Levu made his land a sacred sanctuary, in gratitude for which the ancient gods vowed that they would work exclusively with his descendants. At any given time only one member of the family held the power of healing, that person being the eldest daughter of a ratai. Upon her death the power was transferred to the eldest daughter of the existing ratai.

Losana Tonoka was in most ways the opposite of Marama. She was younger by twenty-five years but still old enough to be treated with respect as a senior person. Tall and slender, she looked like a hungry hawk, an appearance that was enhanced by her large hooked nose, a genetic inheritance from Fatima, the widow of an Afghan camel driver. Fatima and her husband had left the aridity of Central Australia, where the husband had a contract to lead a camel train supplying the vast and dispersed stations there, and were en route to a new life in Chile when their ship ran aground on a reef off the coast of Thangilamba. The then ratai of Tumunu took Fatima, the only survivor, under his protection. He was initially impressed and eventually smitten by her hooked nose, so different from the broad, flat organs that characterised the generality of Tipotans; he spent hours watching and admiring Fatima's lovely proboscis and, incidentally, her other bodily protuberances. In time he composed a lyrical ode referring to her nostrils as 'the twin gateways to heaven' and as 'outlets of the soul's perfume'. In search of this spiritual scent the ratai eventually won entry and re-entry into heaven, not by way of Fatima's nostrils, God forbid, but through a more accommodating portal, from which Losana's grandfather emerged nine months after the initial admission. And, to the ratai's great and enormous happiness, the child had his mother's nose.

It was also a family tradition that the holder of the faith-healing power must be single and virginal. Before her installation, and knowing quite well what was in store for her, Losana followed in the footsteps of past healers in the family by setting out at a tender age to enjoy to the full the decadent delights of the flesh. She became a ferocious man-eater, possessed of an insatiable carnal appetite. As she was fond of saying in later years, referring to particular respectable men, especially the pillars of their communities, 'I used to gobble him up and vice versa.' But upon her elevation at the still randy age of thirty-five, she was pronounced a virgin, a claim that no one dared dispute loudly or otherwise on account of her high rank and close association with the great spirits who had restored her maidenhead.

She remained single and with great difficulty maintained her chastity. Which explained her hungry, hawkish demeanour.

The first International Conference on the Promotion of Understanding and Co-operation Between Modern and Traditional Sciences of Medicine, to which Losana Tonoka and Marama Kakase were invited as participants, was held at the newly constructed Hula Skirt Convention Centre, an annex of Hotel Paradesia. Co-sponsored by the World Health Commission (WHC), the Third Millenium Foundation and the Government of Tipota, it attracted from all corners of the globe over two thousand doctors, psychiatrists, pharmacists, faith-healers, shamans, herbal curers, midwives, masseurs, sorcerers, acupuncturists, Christian Scientists, psychologists, anthropologists and sociologists. There was no American delegation, as the United States was boycotting the conference on the ground that the WHC had allegedly sponsored a communist-inspired conspiracy to destroy the American pharmaceutical industry and the God-given right for free enterprise by disseminating the anyway totally unfounded allegation that Americans were flooding the Third World with dangerous drugs no longer allowed to be sold within their own borders.

Dr Kati Kanikani, the Tipotan Minister for Health, who had relentlessly waged a twenty-year battle against what he called the 'fraudulent malpractices of witch-doctors thriving on the abysmal ignorance of their superstitious fellow men', delivered the opening address at the conference, praising the WHC and the TMF for their historic initiative in bringing together for the first time ever, the modern and the traditional sciences of medicine for the benefit of people everywhere. Dr Kanikani had initially violently opposed giving any kind of recognition to witch-doctors but was compelled by his Prime Minister, the incomparable Ratai Mboso Tawamundu, not only to make his Ministry's facilities and personnel available to the organisers

26

of the conference but also to deliver the opening address. Being an upholder of things from the hallowed past, the Prime Minister was a believer in and promotor of traditional medicine. And being a man of great sagacity, he had cultivated on his lands all the known medicinal trees, shrubs and vines, and had made all these available freely to anyone who needed them. This was no mean factor in his astounding popularity throughout Tipota. He was a friendly, honest and mild-mannered politician. 'Give the most sincere and convincing speech you've ever made,' he told Dr Kanikani. 'Make them believe that you believe or you'll find your bloody arse on the back benches. Good boy.'

Dr Kanikani ordered his Permanent Secretary, under threats of being transferred to the Ministry for Women's Affairs, to write for him the best speech he'd ever written. And the Permanent Secretary told the Director of Hospital Services to write the most sincere and honest speech he had ever written. 'Do it real good,' he said gently, 'or someone's missus'll hear someone's been screwing the matron all these years. Right?' No one knew what the Director of Hospital Services in fact did, for he and the Permanent Secretary were also adamantly opposed to witch-doctors, but on the opening day of the conference Dr Kanikani received what he had ordered and proceeded to deliver the best speech of his career, surprising himself and immeasurably impressing everyone else with his eloquence, sincerity and humanity. Tears of pride and joy streamed copiously down the face of every Tipotan present, most of all Losana and Marama as they sat enthralled by the resonant beauty of the Minister's voice and the sheer poetry of his delivery. Goodness me, he sounds exactly like he used to every time he was about to gobble me up and vice versa, Losana reminded herself over and over during the performance.

'Today,' the Minister concluded, 'we witness in this consecrated hall the birth of the dawn of a new era in the history of humankind, an era in which the modern and traditional sciences of medicine have combined and have indeed united in the bliss of a holy matrimony that will remain unsullied and unsevered for all eternity in order to wage relentlessly the greatest crusade ever mounted for the total elimination and obliteration of all germs that, since before history began, have grautitously, maliciously, obscenely and brutally, tortured, maimed and murdered countless innocent lives of men, women and children of all places, of every colour, creed and nationality.

'Henceforth from today, until total and complete victory is ours and until the enemy is vanquished and consigned to the garbage heap of history, doctors and witch-doctors, therapists and sorcerers, psychiatrists and shamans, and all men and women in their various capacities and stations in life, united in their common love of peace and healthy concourse, must pledge their lives, and those of their descendants for generations to come, and forever if necessary, to courageously, fearlessly and stead-fastly stand side by side and back to back in conducting the glorious battle against the forces of pain and perfidy.

'It is therefore a great privilege and honour for me to declare on the behalf of all humankind, the next one hundred years as the Century for Anti-Germ Warfare.

'Finally, I wish to reveal to each and everyone in this hall, in this country and indeed in this wide, wide world, that our beloved leader, Prime Minister Ratai Mboso Tawamundu, com-bines in his exalted, aristocratic self, the greatest virtues that modernism and traditionalism ever assembled in the person of a single human being. He, our revered leader, may he reign for-ever, and is most likely to, the foremost advocate of the tradi-tional modes of medical practices, is simultaneously the greatest promoter of the development of modern health facilities and ser-vices for all law-abiding and not-so-law-abiding citizens of our treasured Tipota, the Crown Jewel of the South Pacific. Our immortal Prime Minister, Ratai Mboso Tawamundu, who has most recently been proclaimed by the Great International Organisation as the Man and Father of the Decade, is the single most important reason why our beloved land of harmony and stability has been selected above all others to host this great meeting of minds. He is the shining beacon by which this con-ference must be guided, illuminated and inspired. Once again, distinguished practitioners and eminent scholars, I humbly offer you my Government's warmest welcome to our Islands in the Sun.' There's no way that crafty old fox gonna get rid of me now, Dr Kanikani muttered to himself as he tidied up the lectern and bowed to the audience.

The resounding response to the Minister's speech was prolonged and deafening. Losana and Marama were loudest in their applause. It was a proud day for all Tipotans gathered in the hall and for those who had been listening to the live broadcast. Everyone was thrilled by eminent foreigners' enthusiastic acknowledgement of the beauty, brilliance and profundity of Dr Kanikani's address. Losana and Marama were deeply moved by the spectacle and rode the crest of the grand emotional wave, although they understood not one single word the Minister had uttered.

By all accounts the conference was an unqualified success. For the scientists it was the first time that they had personally met those whom they had always dismissed as poseurs and crackpots. Although they would not be parted from their reservations, they openly admitted that without traditional curers the vast majority of the world's population would have no medical attention whatsoever. It was too expensive for modern medicine to cater for everyone. It was good therefore to know that the poor were looking after the poor. This must be encouraged. Different classes and groups of people must find their own levels in everything, including medicine. With this understanding, everyone went out of their way to be pleasant to traditional medical practitioners. And everyone agreed that they would all meet again in the near future in an expenses-paid, follow-up conference in Nairobi to cement the friendships and understanding among all medical practitioners. In the whole conference, there was hardly anything said about the sick and the diseased.

The most satisfied participants were, however, the practitioners of traditional medicine, most of whom could not speak English or French and could not therefore contribute anything to the proceedings of the conference apart from their token presence. For them, the *per diem* allowance of eighty dollars and an honorarium of five hundred dollars was many times more than they had earned in years of toil. Most of all, they were elated by their new recognition as professionals. One of the recommendations that emerged was that the governments of the world should further promote traditional medicine by paying its practitioners fair salaries if employed by the state or, if in private practice, they should receive fees in cash as their remuneration.

The Voice of Tipota aired a series of interviews with selected visitors and local participants. 'What do you think of the conference?' the interviewer asked Dr James Hamilton of the United Kingdom.

'It was a great symbolic success, definitely,' the inebriated physician replied.

'Would you care to elaborate on that?'

'Certainly, one ought to, yes. Er . . . I mean symbolic of the great co-operative spirit that transcends professional and national boundaries. By bringing together hundreds of people with diverse beliefs and practices the conference created profound understanding of the complexity of the field of medicine.'

'I understand that the conference decided to call traditional practitioners "doctors". What do you think of that?'

'Jolly good, that. They deserve to be recognised for the tremendous work they do for mankind. But we have decided to make a clear distinction between the two to avoid confusion.'

'How would you do it, Dr Hamilton?'

'Quite easy, really. It's a simple matter of pronunciation. When you refer to our lot you simply say "doctor" as usual. With the other kind you pronounce it in italics.'

'What do you mean?'

'You say "*dottore*". Sounds very italics, doesn't it?'

'Most interesting indeed. Listeners, from now on you should call our curers *dottores*, the italics pronunciation for doctors. One last question, Dr Hamilton. Were there other significant resolutions made by the conference?'

'I can't remember offhand. However, at the plenary session the Secretary-General of the WHC announced the imminent opening of the International School of Traditional Medicine on Nanggaralevu, an island in Fiji, where established and rising *dottores* will go to study for periods up to two years to bring them up to date and to broaden their fields of competence. Many participants are going to the island for the opening. I'll be there too. This will be a major leap forward in the development of health service for the entire human race. The funding for this institution will come mostly from the Third Millenium Foundation. The necessary facilities are already in place since the island was a major tourist resort before it was bought by the foundation.'

'Thank you, Dr Hamilton. I wish you a happy trip home. And now listeners, we have Losana Tonoka and Marama Kakase, our two notable witch-doctors, er, *dottores*, who participated in the conference.' The interviewer switched to the native language.

'Marama, what is your assessment of the conference?'

'Fantastic! Simply marvellous. The food was out of this world. And the money, er, I mean the many people one met were fabulous. And the money, er, excuse me, although we couldn't speak a word to one another our souls interacted splendidly, you see. It's what the money, damn it, excuse me, what my grandchildren call the vibes and the chemistry. You could feel them. Everything was just right. Enjoyed every minute of it. Losana and I have been invited to a follow-up conference in Naibibi or some such place in Europe very soon.'

'I note that you used the word "money" several times. Have you got anything to say about it?'

'Fantastic! Er, I mean money was of least importance. I can't imagine why it's been on my lips. It's the last thing that should enter one's mind. But conferences like this could spoil one if one allows them to, you know. One must always guard oneself or one becomes mercenary like all those professional conference-goers.'

'Thank you, Marama. Losana, what has been your most memorable experience at the conference?'

'Undoubtedly my meeting with the Afghan doctor. Oh dear, it stirred something in me I never thought was there. He's so handsome. Looks almost exactly like the picture of my grandfather in his younger days. He's got the family nose and eyes. Had we been able to converse we would definitely have compared genealogies. I'm sure there's a connection somewhere there. I can feel it deep down in my soul.'

'Yes, that I can see. What do you think of the recommendations?'

'I didn't understand them all. Only one or two that Dr Tauvi
Mate explained to us later. He sometimes interpreted for us.
He's very nice and kind. But most of the time Marama and I
just sat there like a pair of stunned mullets. No one bothered
to speak to us. How could they? But they were all very kind
though. Smiled and patted us on the back or shook our hands
and stuff. I'm not complaining. They have invited us to Nairobi.
And the money was good, very.'

'How much did you get?'

'I'm not good at counting,' Losana responded with a disarm-
ing fib. 'But it was quite different from what we expected. Quite.
I hear that our situation will soon improve with our recognition
as professionals and our collaboration with our more uppity col-
leagues. I love our new title, *dottore*. Sounds much better than
witch-doctor and such.'

'Do you wish to add anything?'

'Yes, just one thing. Marama and I have been invited by a
remarkable white-haired, white-bearded gentleman, Baba something, to go to Fiji next week for the opening of the International School of Traditional Medicine. We will be away for one
year as trainees at the school. From there we'll go to the follow-
up conference in Nairobi before returning home. Life's so
exciting right now I wish I were still young.'

With her newly acquired wealth Marama hired a taxi to take
her, Losana, Dr Hamilton and Dr Tauvi Mate back to
Korodamu. Hamilton, who had deferred his return home in order
to go to Nanggaralevu, had struck up friendship with Tauvi Mate
and through him with Marama and Losana. Upon hearing that
Losana was to see a patient in Korodamu, he asked if he could
go along to witness at first hand faith-healing in action. Since
he had not seen it done before he was eager to take the opportunity, especially in such a congenial company. He was quick
to assure everyone that his role would strictly be as an interested
observer; Dr Mate had volunteered to accompany him as his
interpreter.

32

Losana was more than happy to have Hamilton tag along. Around thirty-five, tall and good looking, Hamilton reminded her of those men in their prime of carnal expertise who had introduced her to joys beyond description. Although much younger than the others and a little younger even than her, Oilei was one such lover. Losana remembered him as one of her best entertainers, and how he usually performed at peak a day or two after a boxing match. He was superbly fit then, so trim for a heavyweight. And what a champion he was; the best Tipota had ever spawned. Such a pity, she told herself as she stared through the cab window, to be knocked down by your own bottom. Still, it'd be nice to see once again those parts that had given her so much pleasure. She quickly banished such thoughts as soon as she became aware of the throbbing in her thighs. It was no longer so very difficult to rid herself of such nonsense since she had been practising for twenty years.

I'm no bloody mandrill in a fucking zoo, Oilei muttered when, from the bedroom, he heard the Englishman's voice and those of his companions. But he was in too much agony to protest loudly for his dignity. Although the five-day wait for Losana was excruciatingly painful, he would not entertain the idea of going to hospital and letting those nurses look up his arse. Many of them were his relatives or the children of his enemies. He would rather die first; in fact, he had contemplated taking his own life but decided that it was the coward's way out, not that of a former champion. He had sworn violently when Makarita told him about Losana, but two days later he relented, for by then he was in such pain that he would try just about anything short of going to hospital.

The knob turned and Losana entered the bedroom, followed by Hamilton, with Tauvi Mate bringing up the rear and closing the door gently behind him. Makarita tiptoed over and stood on the other side of the door, listening in. Losana bussed Oilei on the cheek and said something the others could not catch. Oilei appeared to be protesting and Losana insisting, but in the end it was he who relented and with much difficulty removed his pyjamas, shifted to one side of the large double bed, turned on his stomach and opened his legs.

Losana climbed on the bed, knelt facing the patient, bent slightly forward and, making circular movements with her hands above Oilei's bared bottom and thighs, announced for everyone, especially Dr Hamilton, to hear, 'There's a very nasty, fat, female devil stuck halfway up your arse trying to back out. As we all know, devils enter the bodies of human beings, playing havoc with them. People thus possessed generally go berserk and do crazy things that most of them would not normally do. Devils usually enter and leave men's bodies through their mouths, the largest of their orifices. But often new devils, who really don't know what's what, try to enter a man's body through the arse when his bottom is raised above his head during acts of copulation or when diving straight down through deep water. Those who enter that way almost always get stuck because the lower orifice is too small. They wriggle and kick a lot, causing tremendous agony, which will not abate until they are released.

'Oilei, you're not a diver because you can't swim. You must have fornicated with someone in the missionary position . . .'

'Not with me!' came a cry from the other side of the door. 'He hasn't done the missionary way on me for months and we haven't done it any other way for weeks! That son of a bitch went out drinking the night before he got the pain in the arse! Serves him right! He must've screwed Caesar on his way back! Don't pull the devil out of his arse. Let the bugger suffer!'

'Tauvi Mate, go and restrain Rita. Get her away from that door, please,' Losana pleaded. Tauvi went out and shortly returned.

'As I said, Oilei. You must've screwed, er, copulated with someone, most probably not your wife and I wouldn't put it past you, or some other creature, which is a horrible thing to do, and while doing it, a new female devil tried to enter you through the wrong end. I can feel her bottom wriggling and her legs kicking.' Losana made movements as if she was trying to hold still a pair of kicking legs.

'But it's my duty to free you from your pain. Our Lord has always been unco-operative in things like this. We'll get Tangaroa, our greatest god, to help us out,' the faith-healer concluded. 'Oh, and another thing. Tangaroa will not pull her out.

He loathes doing it that way. He will push her in and chase her out the right way, through your mouth. You'll certainly hear her making her exit.'

Having said that, Losana traced her right index finger slowly down Oilei's spine until it had disappeared into his buttocks, where it poised at the anal opening. The two witnesses stood perfectly still at the door, doing their best to remain invisible. Maintaining the posture that she had assumed, Losana chanted her incantation in an eerily rich contralto voice:

> Tangaroa dwells in the sky
> Tangaroa dwells in the ocean
>   Mana!
> Tangaroa scales the highest
> Tangaroa dives the deepest
>   Mana!
> Tangaroa breathes in steam
> Tangaroa breathes out fire
>   Mana!
> He knows the dwelling places
> Of good and evil spirits
>   Mana!
> Come Tangaroa, come
> Quickly, Tangaroa, quickly
>   Mana!
> Chase this nasty devil trapped
> In the arse of a mortal man
>   Mana, eeee yah!
>   Mana, eeee yoh!
>   Mana, waa waa
>   HAAA!!!

With that loud and mighty finale, Losana, whose forefinger was still poised at the anal entrance, jabbed it sharply into the hole to expel the devil. 'Mangai Tsinamu!! Fuck your father!!' Oilei screamed at the top of his voice, sprang out of the bed to free himself of Losana's digit, fell heavily on the floor and passed out.

'That was the devil escaping through his mouth,' Losana announced calmly. 'He should be all right in a little while.'

35

But Dr Hamilton had already dashed out into the lounge. He returned promptly with a black bag, knelt beside Oilei, checked his eyes, looked into his mouth and felt his pulse. Satisfied, he prepared a syringe and injected Oilei in the arm. Then he lifted and laid him gently on the bed and covered his nakedness. He sat down on the only chair in the room and waited. Losana and Tauvi were already in the lounge trying to reassure Makarita and her mother.

About half an hour later Dr Hamilton emerged from the bed-room and, looking at Makarita, said, 'He's all right for the moment. Resting peacefully. I've left some tablets in there. Make sure he takes them regularly. Read the instructions carefully. I'd send him to hospital immediately if I were you. He needs an operation soon or it'll get worse. I've had more than enough for the day. I'm going back to town. Thank you for having me here. I shall not forget this experience. Not for a long time.' Without further ado he left, followed by Tauvi Mate.

Oilei was fast asleep and breathing easily when the women stole into the bedroom. He looked so rested and relaxed for the first time in many days that Makarita, in the age-old tradition of Tipotan women quickly forgiving the manifold infidelities of their men, broke down sobbing with relief. The other women returned to the lounge. In a little while Makarita checked the bedside table and found two packets, one of pain-killing tablets, the other some kind of antibiotics. She stood looking at Oilei before kissing his forehead lightly and leaving the room.

'He should've left Oilei well alone,' Losana was saying crossly. 'He promised that he'd do nothing. Never trust those interfering foreigners ever again. No doubt whatever my treatment was working. I saw the devil leave through his mouth. But the Englishman cut in. Now he'll claim the credit.'

'Quite so,' Marama agreed. 'We do our best to cure them and when they start getting better, off they go to someone else. And later claim to have been cured by another's medicine. Stupid ingrates. I simply refuse to treat such people again. They'd come crawling back but I wouldn't talk to them. Anyway, we'd better go. You'll be just in time to catch the bus. Rita, let me know if anything happens again.'

As they were leaving, Makarita slipped a sealed envelope into Losana's hand. She saw them out then went back looking for her mother, who was peeling taro in the kitchen.

'What did you think of that, Mother?'

'Hard to tell. If Oilei recovers, Losana will claim credit; if he doesn't she'll blame the Englishman. I always believe in using more than one kind of medicine. If one fails, others may work. Or they could reinforce one another. You can never tell which kind does the trick. I never really bother trying to find out. As long as I recover, that's all that matters. Main thing is to get well. Did the doctor leave any medicine?'

'Yes. And I'll give it to him regularly.'

'Good. Don't take Marama too seriously. Always hedge your bets and you'll be fine.'

Oilei woke up in the dark, vaguely remembering stirring once and taking tablets. The agony had all but disappeared, although he felt rather raw where Losana had jabbed. That was nothing compared with what he had endured in the previous days. But his sense of relief evaporated when he became aware of something he had not felt since he was a little boy. I must've wet the bed, he thought as he switched on the light to check. The whole area his bottom had occupied was covered with blood and pus. His pyjamas were in a mess.

'Rita! Rita!' he called as he got off the bed.

Makarita dashed in from the lounge, where she had been taking turns with Mere in case Oilei needed help. She braked in her tracks when she saw what was going on.

'Good heavens! Are we menstruating or what?'

'It's not funny. I bled from behind. Get some cotton wool, will you? I'm still bleeding. Hurry up.'

Makarita returned with a packet of Modess. 'I said cotton wool, for Chrissake! What do you think I am, a fucking woman?' Oilei raged.

'Don't shout at me or you look for it yourself. There isn't any.'

'Then get some from the shop. Use your bloody brain for once. Gawd!'

'It's three in the morning, you stupid oaf. I'll go when the shops open. Try this, for heaven's sake. No one's looking.'

With an utter lack of grace Oilei grabbed the packet, tore it, got out a pad and wiped his bottom. The pad soaked through immediately. He threw it on the floor, grabbed a handful and stuffed them in. These also became saturated. Soon he ran out of pads.

'Better go to the toilet,' Makarita suggested, 'and stay there. There aren't any more pads. How's the pain?'

'Forget the bloody pain. I'm bleeding to death. Dear Lord. If it's not one thing it's another. I'll flush myself down the bloody loo, I'm telling you,' he announced bitterly as he made his way to the door like someone carrying a half-deflated soccer ball between his legs.

'Let me get in there first. Just for a pee, please,' Makarita pleaded. 'I'm desperate.'

'Over my dead body. Do it outside, for Chrissake. It's dark. No one's looking.'

He entered the toilet, leaving the door open, and made himself comfortable. Makarita was in action under the bush just outside the toilet window: a mighty long weewee that hissed like a leaky faucet.

Then her indignant voice crashed through, 'Caesar! You bloody pervert, go pee somewhere else!'

A sharp blow, a painful yelp and Makarita stalked inside. 'You'd better get rid of that animal of yours. He's bound to rape someone sooner or later.'

'It won't be you, that's for certain. He's choosy, old Caesar is,' Oilei chuckled.

'You should laugh, huh!' but despite herself, Makarita broke up. The bugger's getting back into his old form.

'It must've been a boil,' Oilei said conversationally.

'What boil?'

'In the arse, that's what. The pain and all that. Now the bleeding. Must've been Losana's finger that pricked the head open.'

'I wouldn't be too sure if I were you. It could equally have been the Englishman. He gave you a shot while you were out. You also took some tablets in the afternoon.'

'No. I don't think so . . . What the hell. It doesn't matter as long as the pain's gone. I'm feeling much better already. Except for the bleeding. Once it's over I'll be quickly on the mend.'

A few days later Losana Tonoka, Marama Kakase and Dr James Hamilton left with a dhoti-clad, white-haired, white-bearded gentleman for Fiji. Oilei was destined not to see them again until months later in another country. As for the gentleman in dhoti, Oilei would see him sooner than that in an encounter that would change the course of his life by introducing him to a movement bent on determining the fate of the human species in the twilight of the twentieth century and the dawn of the Third Millenium.

3

There was now no problem for patients in Tipota in finding *dottores* to attend to them. People had only to listen to the radio or read the daily press to discover who was operating and where. Most of those advertising were newcomers with no family tradition in medicine, but who had only just received strange and mystical revelations that they had curative powers. The old-established *dottores* operated in their traditional ways, shunning modern publicity media and contemptuously dismissing the new breed as rootless upstarts and impostors.

The sudden public prominence of the new class of *dottores* and the increasing interest in non-modern medicine developed from a confluence of many events. First and foremost in triggering curiosity and interest was the media publicity given to the recognition of traditional medicine and its practitioners by the World Health Council and the Tipotan Government. The Minister for Health's opening address at the historic conference had made him a national hero and an instant international celebrity. Dr Kanikani had since been invited to deliver keynote speeches to several conferences of a similar kind all over the world, and to undertake gruelling international lecture and media tours. Back home, he had left instructions that all assistance be provided by his Ministry to facilitate the development of traditional medicine. He was also appointed chairman of the board of governors of the newly established International School of Traditional Medicine and had thrice visited it in the company of a white-haired, white-bearded gentleman wearing dhoti.

The collapse of the national development policies also contributed to the rise of interest in traditional medicine. As joblessness rose throughout the nation, the new propaganda sloganeering focused on self-employment, for neither the public nor the private sector could provide any more jobs for anyone. In fact, retrenchment was the order of the day. The practice of traditional medicine was seen as one avenue for self-employment.

Rising inflation had, moreover, taken most available pharmaceutical drugs and private doctors out of reach of the vast majority of the population, the most vulnerable section of the community to disease. This large group had perforce to look to traditional medicine for succour.

A combination of the perennial shortages in essential drugs and in experienced doctors, most of whom had emigrated to the greener fields of Australia, Canada and the United States, had left the hospitals poorly supplied and undermanned. At the same time there was an alarming increase in the reported rate of mortality in hospitals, blamed by the public on negligence and incompetence on the part of doctors. Most ordinary Tipotans avoided their hospitals as if they were morgues. Of particular interest to Oilei, and this sealed his resolve not to enter hospital, was a press report of a man who had sued the General Hospital for an error in an operation on his arse that had left him totally incontinent. When this case was first heard in the Supreme Court the patient entered carrying a chamber pot, which he placed on the floor right in front and sat on it after he had pulled down his pants. The judge took the dimmest view of the matter, but after a heart-rending explanation by the plaintiff's solicitor His Honour turned his wrathful countenance upon the superintendent of the General Hospital and the Crown Solicitor and said most balefully, 'I have in mind to order that the pair of you be carved in the way that you butchered this wretched victim of your gross incompetence.'

Finally, but not least, there was a dearth of sensational events for media interest. The Parliament was in recess and most of the time the Prime Minister and most of the senior Cabinet Ministers were away overseas playing golf and soliciting aid funds, while the six leaders of the Opposition (it was the only political party in the entire world that had half a dozen leaders of equal rank) were also overseas playing golf and plotting one another's downfall instead of the Government's. Because of the

41

economic recession, businessmen and civil servants had little worth embezzling, and burglars found it a waste of time to steal property they could not dispose of quickly and safely. There was also a shortage of beer, owing to a prolonged strike by brewery workers, resulting in a marked decline in alcohol-related crimes such as wife bashing, child abuse, gang rape, street brawls, road accidents, murder and other familiar daily occurrences that would normally fill half the space and time of the daily press and the airwaves. In search of newsworthy events, journalists descended upon the new breed of entrepreneurs, the miracle *dottores*, and in doing so raised the general interest of a desperate and gullible public in their activities.

Oilei was still bleeding, although the flow was considerably less. He had resigned himself to wearing cotton pads, changing them several times a day. He now understood in part what it was like to be a woman. The pain had returned to plague him after the tablets left by Dr Hamilton had all been taken. Through Tauvi Mate he obtained from the General Hospital more pain-killers, which offered him no relief since they were long past their expiry date. It was useless trying to get any decent medicine from the chemists in town as they had been boycotting the Government-owned Central Pharmaceutical Depot, an agency with a total monopoly on drug import and distribution.

After his unfortunate experiences with long-established healers, Oilei, like thousands of his fellow Tipotans, consulted one miracle *dottore* after another, rapidly diminishing his financial and farm resources and finding no respite from his pain or his bleeding, even though many others, including those with a pain in the arse, declared that they had been relieved of their suffering.

During one of his visits to a new-breed *dottore* he almost brought disaster upon himself as well as the healer. The *dottore* was Domoni Thimailomalangi of Davui, a village thirty kilometres from Korodamu. Domoni had been a garbage collector in Kuruti for fifteen years when he went home as he did every Christmas for his three-week vacation. On Boxing Day, as accounts relate, he was walking along a beach a short distance from his village when he heard a soft voice calling him. He looked around but saw no one. Then he looked down and observed a large conch shell near his feet, picked it up, and, finding a ready-made hole near the tail end, blew into it with all his strength. The sound produced was the best he had heard from a conch shell. When he finished blowing he heard his name being called again, and to his utter surprise the voice was coming through the mouth of the shell. 'Domoni,' it said, 'go and tell Maria to get up.' Though frightened by the experience, he obeyed, taking the shell with him. Maria, his elder sister, had been in bed for nearly five years suffering from a form of paralysis attributed by the villagers to punishment by displeased ancestral spirits.

Domoni entered Maria's house to find it filled with a group of women visiting her for prayer. While they were praying he tiptoed into their midst, raised the shell and blew. As the startled ladies opened their eyes Domoni pointed a finger at his sister and commanded, 'Get up, Maria!' So surprised was she that, not realising what she was doing, Maria jumped up and walked to her brother. The other women were so impressed that they broke out singing hymns of praise. Those who had sick relatives hurried home and brought them to Domoni. By the following day word had spread to other villages and people began flocking in. The media were informed and the resulting publicity drew crowds from every corner of Tipota and even abroad.

By the end of his first week of practice Domoni had developed a method of healing that was very simple and utterly revolutionary. He placed the mouth of the conch shell very close to his patient's diseased part, organ, or member and blew it until the sufferer started humming a tune that he or she heard coming from the shell. Although the actual sound of the conch shell was tuneless, it magically transformed itself into music when it entered the patient's brain. Every sufferer heard a different tune, each of which had the power to heal. As soon as a patient heard his tune and started humming he was on the road to recovery; he went away and hummed every three minutes until all signs of his complaint had disappeared. Domoni was dubbed the Conch Shell Miracle Music Man.

Domoni's treatment soon set the entire Tipotan population humming for the whole thing was so infectious that even healthy people hummed along as a preventative. Although hummers hummed different pieces of music, the tunes somehow synchronised and harmonised so beautifully and so melodiously that, for the two months in which Domoni practised, the whole country was at peace with itself for the first time in history. Even politicians stopped telling lies to the nation, and multinational firms and other business houses reduced their prices by ninety per cent and still made hefty profits.

When Oilei stepped off the bus at Davui to consult Domoni he found thousands of people sitting under makeshift shelters and trees, humming and drinking kava while groups of humming women busied themselves cooking for the gathering. The raw food was brought by the patients as gifts for Domoni. These offerings, which often included traditional valuables such as mats and tapa cloth, were always called gifts because *dottores* never charged fees for their services. Although they could perform without offerings as they occasionally did, very few of their patients went to them empty-handed, for gifts were an integral part of the curing process.

In Domoni's case, visiting patients and their escorts of relatives were in such hummingly euphoric states they brought him as many gifts as they could carry or transport, the result being that there was always more than sufficient food to cater for everyone, including the entire population of Davui and neighbouring villages. In fact, most members of these communities stopped working in their gardens to sit around in Davui singing their hero's praise and freeloading on what their visitors brought.

Since he was a national figure, Oilei was instantly recognised and at once ushered into a round hut in which Domoni dealt with his patients. The conical roof of the hut was supported by a central post and smaller ones around the wall.

'Sir, I'm greatly honoured by your visit,' Domoni greeted his famous patient. 'I've heard about your problem and have been wondering whether you'd think of trying the power of my shell.'

'Sir, I'm greatly honoured by your very kind reception,' Oilei responded. 'My problem's causing me a great deal of pain and suffering.'

'Be comforted, Oilei Bomboki, your problem will be history as soon as you start humming a magical tune. Please remove your pants and bend forward.'

Oilei complied and Domoni sat on the floor, plugged a mute into the mouth of the conch shell, held it almost against Oilei's bottom and blew. Five minutes later he paused and asked rather testily, 'Why aren't you humming?'

'I haven't heard my tune yet,' Oilei replied.

'You should've heard it by the end of the first minute. Everyone does. Now concentrate, please.' And Domoni blew again for three minutes, by which time he was almost breathless and just about to give up when the miracle happened. The hum came from Oilei's blowhole. It came forth sounding like the high note of a Stradivarius, or someone trying to muffle a fart during church service. There was no mistaking the fact that Oilei was squeezing out a hauntingly beautiful tune, which not even the great Amadeus would have dreamed up for a flute concerto.

'This has never happened in the entire history of mankind,' said Domoni, doing his very best to control himself.

'It certainly has never happened to me before. And I'm not leaving here farting music all over the fucking place. Do something.'

'Right. We'll try again. Next time you hum through the correct orifice. OK?'

Domoni removed the mute from the conch shell, held its mouth a few millimetres from Oilei's bottom, took a deep breath and blew with all his might. The mighty sound reverberated around the small single-room hut so that it shook. Oilei felt it enter his arse and travel through into his stomach, stirring his innards as it got mixed up with methane gas. Domoni stopped and asked breathlessly, 'Have you got the tune?'

'Not yet. But I can hear rumbling in my tummy.'

'Forget the fucking rumbling. Concentrate!'

He resumed blowing. Oilei felt his stomach inflating and stretching tight before everything rushed backward like a retreating tornado. It shot out into the loudest fart he had exploded to date, crashed head-on with the point-blank blast from the conch shell, and the resulting thunderclap shattered the instrument, bowled Domoni over backward and knocked the still bending Oilei forward, smashing his head against the base of the centre post. People rushed in to find their beloved *dottore* out cold with his lacerated face splattered all over with shards of the conch shell; Oilei was also unconscious, his bleeding pate stopping against the base of the post and his bare bum sticking up into the air.

Almost an hour later the victims revived. Oilei rose, summoned as much of his tattered dignity as he could and staggered out to the bus stop, his arse throbbing with pain. As for Domoni Thimailomalangi, the destruction of his magical instrument shattered his promising career.

Oilei tried other *dottores* without avail. Word spread throughout Tipotan medical circles that his was the most difficult arse to handle. It became a matter of challenge for miracle *dottores* to apply their skills and powers to an orifice that had consistently defied the wisdom of the ages. One *dottore* after another fell foul of Oilei's orifice, and since certain journalists had taken upon themselves to monitor his progress and report on it, reputations were destroyed and many curers went out of business as a direct result. Some did so quietly while others, like Domoni, crashed spectacularly.

Unknown to Oilei, however, one of those who followed his progress closely was an old white-haired, white-bearded gentleman wearing dhoti, who went around offering a one-year fellowship to every fallen *dottore* to study at the International School of Traditional Medicine at Nanggaralevu in Fiji. Clutching at any straw that offered them a chance for the restoration of their powers, felled *dottores* such as Domoni Thimailomalangi accepted the fellowship and went. No one at the time appreciated the regional and global significance of the old man's activities.

Only one *dottore* who confronted Oilei's troubled organ emerged from the encounter with his reputation intact. He was Amini Sese, who came from Vonu, a coastal village located between the two biggest international resort hotels in Tipota, and about three kilometres from each. The whole coastline of about sixty kilometres was dotted by many other hotels, the area being the tourist centre for the country because of its beaches and relatively dry climate. It was known the world over as the Sunshine Coast.

Amini was a degree graduate of the University of the Southern Paradise who emerged at the end of his studies to find that there was no job for him anywhere. He went back to his parents but found no solace there either. In his despondency he decided one day to swim out into the ocean and offer his body and brain to the sharks, since no one else wanted them. He was seen in the act by some children who ignored him, thinking that he was taking a long swim, until his parents started inquiring about his whereabouts.

Three or so kilometres out into the ocean it became clear to Amini that the sharks and the barracudas did not want him either, so he started swimming back. But by then he was exhausted and was on the verge of drowning. He saw a lifeboat drifting toward him and, with his remaining strength and a new will to survive, he stroked toward the craft, hauled himself in and collapsed into insensibility. He woke up when he was jolted by the boat hitting hard surface. Although it was dark, he recognised that he had landed on the beach in front of his village.

It was also then that he noticed to his utter amazement that his craft was not a lifeboat or any other kind of boat but the enormous shell of what must have been a giant turtle. Amini sat down and stared at it in wonderment for several hours before the idea occurred to him. He recalled Domoni Thimailomalangi's discovery of the miracle conch shell and his subsequent rise to national prominence. Well, well! he said to himself. If a mere garbage collector could take a whole nation in with a little washed-up shell, then he, Amini Sese, Bachelor of Arts from the greatest Centre of Excellence in the South Pacific, could do much better with what was undoubtedly the shell of the largest turtle the world's oceans had ever nourished. As he thought along this line, all the theories coalesced that he had learnt in Creative Accounting and Sociology, his two majors, and the outline of a brilliant plan emerged. He patted the rim of the shell and said with great confidence, 'The Future's Ours, Comrade,' quoting the motto of the University of the Southern Paradise.

Amini collected some flying phosphorescent insects and rubbed them on his legs so that they lit up. Then in a low voice he tried out a hair-raising call that he had heard in movies until he was certain that he could do it full blast. When all was ready, he carried the shell to the middle of the village green, put it down and, in a terrifyingly piercing voice, released the Tarzan call for fifteen seconds and went under the shell.

People came out of their houses to see what was happening. Someone swept the green with a six-battery torch and stopped it on a large object making what appeared to be very odd movements. Other torches focused on the object as they converged upon it. They were all stunned and awed by the sheer size of the shell; they had never seen a turtle shell half as big. 'How did it get here? Who brought it?' someone asked. But before anyone could answer, the shell rose and two glowing legs appeared and moved. They scattered in all directions, men, women and children, all screaming and speaking in tongues. The shell walked towards Amini's parents' wooden house. As it climbed up the front steps his father, mother, brothers, sisters and a host of relatives who had gathered to mourn his death, screamed and stampeded through the back door or jumped out of windows. Amini negotiated the shell through the doorway and placed it in the middle of the hastily vacated living room.

When the village had quietened down, Amini stood on top of the front steps and gave another Tarzan call before he spoke in a loud, booming voice.

'Pay attention! Pay attention! Listen carefully to me. I'm Amini Sese, your son and brother whom you have given up for dead. During the day our mighty sea god, the eight-headed Toke Moana, led me into the middle of the Pacific Ocean, where the spirit of the great turtle, Sangone, took me into his shell to guide him back home to Tipota. As some of you know, Sangone was stolen from us centuries ago by the Fijians, then by the thieving Samoans from the larcenous Fijians, and finally by the dirty Tongans from the filthy Samoans. Those bloody Tongans imprisoned the poor, innocent Sangone in a cave guarded by their most cannibalistic devils. Sangone died of a broken heart but his spirit lived on, weeping in his shell by the rivers of Babylon, so to speak, biding his time to free himself and come home, sweet home. Three weeks ago, after a thousand-year captivity, Sangone tricked his stupid guards and escaped, sailing sweet homeward bound in his mighty shell. To cut the story short, so as not to make too much song and dance, or build mountains out of molehills, or sing my own praises, let me announce to one and all, that as from tonight, from this very minute in time and space, and until further notice, Sangone has appointed me his emissary and prophet to spread the good word, to heal the sick, make the blind see, the drunk sober, the deaf to hear, the dumb to speak, the lame to run and the moronic to understand. Fathers, mothers, brothers and sisters, comrades all, spread the good news that tomorrow at noon the Sangone Health Resort will open for business! Cheers and shalom to all! Hip, hip, hooray!!'

Patients began arriving the following noon and Amini dealt with them individually, invisible under the huge turtle shell like a priest in a confessional. The front end of the shell was propped up on a log enabling Amini to reach out and touch the patients' troubled parts, organs or members as he chanted a prayer in a tongue no one understood. From the time of his return from the ocean Amini was never seen again by anyone except the members of his immediate family. His invisibility added an aura of mystery to his person.

Within a month, and after the media had spread Amini's fame, a tent city mushroomed in and around Vonu. Army tents donated by foreign governments for hurricane relief somehow found their way to the village. People came by the hundreds and thousands from the length and breadth of Tipota to seek relief or to marvel at the giant shell. A sense of an almost messianic expectation pervaded the area, but since there was no attempt to convert people to any religion the atmosphere was festive.

By then Amini could not cope with each patient individually. He had people grouped according to the nature of their complaints and dealt with them en masse. Patients held on to a long rope, one end of which rested in the shell. When Amini chanted his prayer he grabbed the rope and transmitted his power through it to every member of the group. As an astute Accounting graduate, Amini sent the foodstuff and handcraft brought by his patients to the main produce markets, including the one at Kuruti, to be sold by his agents, thus earning for himself an income far greater than what he would have got as an employee.

The large crowds of people moving in and out of the festive atmosphere of the vastly expanded village attracted curious tourists from the nearby resort hotels and eventually from the whole Sunshine Coast. All along Amini had anticipated this. One day tourists confronted a large sign at the entrance to the village that read, 'Welcome to the Healing Waters of Sangone's Spa', and on a corner below, 'Fifty cents an hour'. On a post adjacent to the sign was nailed an arrow pointing to the beach in front of the village. Curiosity drove some of the tourists to pay the fee and try the water. They were most pleasantly surprised by its cool, fresh nature, so markedly different from the very salty, tepid sea along the rest of the Sunshine Coast. The explanation for this was that just below the high-water mark there were many freshwater springs flowing into the lagoon. Geologists said that they were outlets of a subterranean river. Word spread fast and tourists with ailments arrived in increasing numbers, most believing that they found some kind of relief.

Once again, and with the support of the Tipota Visitors Bureau, the media publicised Sangone's Spa internationally, and in no time the sick and the diseased in body and mind poured in from the richest regions of the world to make Vonu both a South Sea tropical paradise and a health centre. Airlines increased their flights to Tipota and the hotels along the Sunshine Coast expanded their facilities to accommodate the visitors. Restaurants and coffee houses soon dotted the waterfront of Vonu and it was no longer necessary to send the local handcrafts anywhere else for sale. The Vonu people themselves produced the most popularly sold souvenirs, the small replicas of Sangone's shell. Almost equally in demand were cassette tapes of Amini's chants. No one, not even the most learned linguists, could say which language Amini used. A whole research unit was established at the university to analyse the tapes, but not one word was remotely related to any other word in any living or extinct tongue. Whenever anyone asked him questions about the words he used, he would answer in the unknown language, thus putting an end to further questions. Partly because of this, people attributed mystical powers to the incomprehensible words he uttered; they even said that the very sounds of the words cured the deaf and the dumb.

Amini's stubborn insistence on his invisibility, despite requests from every quarter that he be seen, soon placed him in the same category as Greta Garbo. The only concession he made to demands that he be more accessible was to order a three-kilometre plastic clothesline that ran from the shell to the beach. At noon every day, and for a period of ten minutes, any foreign visitor who wished to feel his powers could close a fist on the line while listening to a taped chant by Amini, who would be holding one end of the line under the shell. Everyone said that they experienced an indescribable something, which entered the innermost part of their being and rested there for a while before it left, taking away all their worries and cares. The *Tipota Herald* quoted an Australian alcoholic who said that the experience was akin to 'being stroked by the tail of eternity'.

So it came to pass that single-handedly, Amini Sese achieved what the combined brains of government departments and the private sector failed miserably to do; that was, to reverse the recessionary trend and usher in a new age of economic prosperity for the country.

But all this came after Amini had dealt with Oilei. The reputation of Oilei's stubbornly resisting arse, and news of the fall of many *dottores* because of their failure to cure him, had already reached Amini by the end of his first month of practice, giving him time to devise a strategy should Oilei show up. Oilei arrived at Vonu in the sixth week, and was given the honour of being individually received.

'So you have come at last,' said the voice from the shell. 'I've been expecting you for some time. For your problem I have medicine that works only on a long-term basis, depending on one's age and metabolism. At your age it'll take effect not less than a year and not more than eighteen months from now. There's no doubt that your illness will be gone by then.'

Amini paused and picked up a half-litre bottle, 'Take that medicine all at once when you get home. From then on it's a matter of patient waiting. Please let me touch the troubled part.'

Oilei presented his bottom; Amini reached out, touched it and chanted a prayer.

'That's all. May God walk with you,' he said, dismissing the patient.

Left alone, Amini sighed with relief. In twelve months he would be so strongly established that any failure, such as the possible one with Oilei, would not affect him in any significant way. By then, he figured (quite accurately as it turned out), Oilei would either have died or been cured by other means. In either case he was safe.

On his way home after leaving Amini, Oilei was very depressed. He had hoped for a quick solution but had instead been given a long-term one. Lately he had developed migraine, as if he had not had enough pain already. He must get some relief soon or he would go insane.

In the following weeks he tried other *dottores* but not one was able to release him from his suffering. He thus had to learn to live with his problem. It was not, however, the sustained agony that he had had to endure initially. Since the abscess started draining there were brief intervals, the longest being half a day, when he was free of pain, but when pain came it lasted several hours, leaving him drained of energy and looking for the most luridly abusive expressions to hurl at everyone. Most people kept away from him. The new pastor, the Reverend Rongo Taratara, had visited him soon after assuming his new position, but since that experience, he told Mere, he preferred praying for Oilei from a safe distance. As a clergyman, he had no difficulty in turning his other cheek or taking personal abuse stoically, but he would never knowingly expose the Saviour to the kind of vile blasphemy he had heard from Oilei.

Oilei had also taken to snapping at Mere, something he had not done before. His mother-in-law had moved in with them to help out and comfort her daughter. She never returned his invective, preferring instead to act as a buffer between husband and wife. But not once in their married life had Oilei physically attacked Makarita, showing a restraint that was quite uncommon among Tipotan men. The idea of hitting her never occurred to him. Makarita knew this very well and took full advantage of it to give as good as she got. They loved, they fought; they had no idea of how else to conduct their relationship.

During one of their fights, triggered by Makarita's suggestion that Oilei start an arse-blood-bank business, Bulbul Bohut knocked loudly on the front door.

'Go away, no one's home!' Oilei shouted.

Bulbul opened the door and walked in. 'Watch your mouth, you son of a bitch,' he scolded pleasantly as he made himself at home.

The remark cleared the air, for Oilei was fond of no one more than Bulbul Bohut. Makarita had also come to like Bulbul, whose visits always brought out the best in Oilei and everyone else in the house. The children, who were then away on scholarships, called him Uncle Bull, which always elicited his playful protests.

Bulbul had first visited Oilei soon after the faith-healing episode and had failed to persuade him to go to the hospital for an operation. From then on he had helped Oilei by driving him in his taxi to various *dottores* all over the island. Now he had come to take Oilei to see an old man, a famed *dottore* who lived on the island of Rovoni about forty kilometres from Korodamu. He was told that the old *dottore* was very famous, very effective and had successfully treated many important people, including Cabinet Ministers and whites.

4

Oilei and Bulbul grew up next door to each other in a depressed part of Kuruti. It was when they started schooling that Oilei took the pint-sized Bulbul under his wings, for there were things about him that attracted other children's fists and feet. Oilei fought everyone who hit or harassed Bulbul, and most of the time he succeeded even against boys older than him. He protected Bulbul through primary and secondary schools, developing on the way the taste for pugilism and the fearlessness that would later take him to the top of the heavyweight division and make him the national and South Pacific champion. From this early relationship grew an unbreakable bond of friendship between himself and Bulbul.

When Oilei took up boxing at the age of nineteen Bulbul became his manager. That was the turning point in their lives. Bulbul had the frugality and the eye-for-the-main-chance acuity of his migrant ancestry, while Oilei displayed the physical prowess and aggression characteristic of the warrior traditions of his forebears. Their partnership was to become an unbeatable and profitable combination. Oilei earned their initial income from his fights; Bulbul banked most of it and adamantly refused to pander to his friend's early tendency towards profligacy. With their savings, for Oilei had never claimed his boxing earnings as his alone, they bought three second-hand cars and started a taxi service, with Bulbul as the financial controller. Oilei used his mouth and fearsome reputation to keep their drivers honest and to convert crooks and muggers into God-fearing upright citizens when dealing with him. They soon added three more second-hand cars to their fleet and became moderately well off, though by no means wealthy.

During this period Oilei met Makarita, a very pretty young

54

teacher who had just begun her career. Oilei was driving an empty taxi slowly past the congested terminal when he saw a girl entering a bus. For some reason, unknown even to himself, he fell for her. It was perhaps the way she held her head or walked that caught him, but whatever it was he fell. Up to then he had not felt deeply for any member of the opposite sex, although he had dallied with many, including the insatiable Losana Tonoka. He had always treated women as playmates to have fun with and move on; there was fortunately no dearth of ladies who held the same views about men. He had no problem in winning them, for as the heavyweight champion he was a household name throughout Tipota. He was also an impressively good-looking man who, at almost two metres, towered over most people. Every schoolgirl reputedly had pictures of him pasted inside the covers of her exercise books.

But as soon as he saw Makarita he surprised himself by saying out loud, 'She's my wife', and instinctively checked the back seat to make sure no one was there. He followed the bus and then tracked Makarita on foot when she alighted at Korodamu. She had no inkling of what was happening and as soon as she reached home, went to clean herself up in a detached bath house at the back.

Oilei confronted the father, a complete stranger, and asked for permission to marry his daughter. Just like that. Makarita's father was a poor man, probably the poorest in the village, on account of his being a drunkard, a habit he had acquired while fighting in Guadalcanal against Hirohito's forces. It was said that he took to drinking on his first day of action, when his battalion was subjected to heavy bombardment by American ships and planes acting under faulty intelligence.

Either because he was soused or was shell-shocked by Oilei's effrontery, Makarita's father merely gaped in response. Mere, who had joined her husband just in time to hear Oilei's proposal, went quickly to the rescue. She, like everyone else, knew Oilei by sight. As a boxer his pictures adorned the walls of just about every house in the country. Later his reputation as the only Tipotan boxer who had saved his earnings and become a successful businessman, spread far and wide. The poor young man who had succeeded in the most masculine sport and had become a rising tycoon, was touted as a model for all youngsters to emulate.

Mere told him that theirs was a very poor, undeserving family, but that she and her ailing husband were deeply touched by his presence in their home and by his honourable intentions towards their beloved daughter, the only jewel from their union. They would have had more girls from whom Oilei could have selected a mate had her dear husband not been rendered incapable by Emperior Hirohito's hordes. On behalf of her husband and of her own self, she would like to extend their welcome and willingness to have him as part of the family.

'But have you talked with her about it? It's a silly question, I know, but as a concerned parent, I must ask it,' Mere asked apologetically.

'As a matter of fact, I have not,' Oilei responded calmly.

'No wonder she hasn't said anything. We're very close, you know. I've always thought we didn't keep secrets from each other. Silly old me, I should have known better. If you haven't talked about it, then you must've talked about other things. So many new things to talk about before people get around to discussing marriage and stuff. People should get to know each other before jumping into, er, I mean, before taking the plunge into the stormy seas of marriage, you know what I mean. Talking about new things is the best way into another's heart . . .'

'No. We haven't talked about any new things.'

'Then you must've been talking about old things, dear old memories, reminiscences and stuff,' Mere started probing.

'As a matter of fact, we haven't talked about those things either.'

'Perhaps you've been taking her sightseeing and things in that lovely automobile of yours?'

'We haven't done that either, as a matter of fact.'

O Lord. 'What have you two been doing all this time?' Mere was getting alarmed.

'Nothing, as a matter of fact. We've done absolutely nothing.'

'Not even a moochy moochy and stuff young things do these days? No? I don't understand. Even in my days we did a little naughty-naughty, not all the way, but you know. Perhaps you could say something about your romance.'

'No I can't . . .'

'Why not?'

'Because there's been no romance. As a matter of fact, I've only been romantic toward her this very day.'

'Oh, that's a relief. So you've been good friends until today. I'm not surprised. It happens all the time. People have been friends for years without knowing the truth about their feelings.'

'True. But you see,' Oilei tried to explain, 'your daughter and I haven't been friends at all.'

'So you've been pretending to be enemies. Hard-to-get games and that sort of thing? I'm not at all surprised. It happens all the time. It's led to some of the best marriages there are.'

'We weren't even enemies, as a matter of fact.'

O Lord. 'Do you know her at all?'

'No and yes . . .'

'You mean yes and no . . .'

'No, as a matter of fact. I mean I don't know her, and yes, I feel that I've known her since eternity. I've been waiting a long, long time for her.'

Help me Lord. 'Do you even know Makarita's name?'

'Now that you've said it, yes.'

'But not before?'

'No . . .'

'You must've seen her at the very least?'

'As a matter of fact, yes.'

'That makes sense. So you've been following her around without talking to her. That also happens all the time.'

'No, as a . . .'

'How many times have you seen her?'

'Only once, as a matter of fact.'

'What?'

'Once. I've said that twice.'

'When was that?'

'Today, as a . . .'

'What?' O merciful Lord. 'When exactly did you see her today?'

57

'About an hour ago, when she boarded the bus.'

'Wait a minute. Are you telling me that the first and only time you've seen my little darling daughter was today when she boarded the bus to come home, and that on that basis you've decided to marry her?'

'As a matter of fact, yes.'

O Lord, forgive my sins. 'Have you really had a good look at her?'

'Not really . . .'

'What?'

'I only looked at her from behind as she boarded . . .'

'What? Didn't you try to look at her face?'

'I would have, but I was in a moving car. Anyway, as far as I'm concerned, seeing her face was not important. It was enough to see her back to know the rest of her and that she's mine. You see, boxing teaches you to assess a person very quickly. When your opponent's warming up in his corner with his back to you, you can tell in a flash what the rest of him's like, his looks, his strength, speed and stuff. It's the same when I saw Makarita's back. She's mine, I said.'

Bloody hell she's yours. 'What if it turns out that she's ugly?'

'Not possible, as a matter of fact.'

Sweet Lord, I'm dealing with a sex maniac. 'So you're set in your mind to marry her?'

'Most definitely, yes. You see, my best friend, Bulbul Bohut, married someone he'd never seen before. At the wedding she was all covered up from head to toe. The whole thing was arranged between the parents. And he didn't even see her for days after the wedding. That's the custom among them. That's why they're so good in business. Risk everything for what they don't know and work like buggery, sorry, to make it a success. At least I have seen a part of your daughter.'

This man's not only a sex maniac but a bloody liar to boot, Mere decided. He's seen Makarita's every little bit and more. But she was completely stumped. There was something about Oilei that she couldn't resist. She eventually sent him away, politely saying that if he really wanted to marry Makarita then he must woo her properly like a good Christian and not like those

58

Hindu heathens. Neither mother nor father believed any word Oilei had uttered apart from his desire to marry their daughter. They were convinced that he and Makarita had fabricated the story to conceal their affair, and that they had decided to marry only because Makarita was pregnant. They had heard of Oilei's famous escapades over the years and could not conceive of a man with his standing and experience falling for someone he had not seen properly.

That night they tried to force a confession from Makarita, who, after failing to convince them of her innocence, closed her mouth tight and sat in defiant silence as they bullied and berated her. They finally decided that for the good name of the family, she must marry her lover. Everyone in the village had seen his car, and him, following her home. It was no good trying to deny it. To stop all the talk she must marry Oilei. Anyway, he was very famous and well off, much better off than anyone in the village. Most girls would throw everything away just to hop into bed with him. Makarita was lucky he had not discarded her as he had done everyone else.

Oilei arrived on the following day and started wooing her like a Christian gentleman, although no one remembered ever having seen him inside a church. From then on for well nigh a whole year he spent most of his spare time as well as much of his working hours in Korodamu. He always went in his taxi, taking presents for Makarita. The car very quickly became a form of free transportation for just about everyone in the village. Bulbul was worried about the effect of all this on their business, but he kept strictly quiet hoping that his friend would soon marry. To expedite this he paid for about half the things Oilei needed for his courtship, while expanding their company's activities by trucking produce from the village to the city market; initially this was to make up for the drop in their taxi earnings, but later it became quite lucrative.

At first Oilei seemed to be courting everyone in Korodamu but Makarita, who refused to acknowledge his existence. When she eventually relented she made life very difficult for him by never giving him a straight answer. 'Maybe' was her favourite response to his invitations, and more often than not she deliberately stood him up. But the more difficult she was, the more enamoured Oilei became of her, demonstrating this by his almost lavish generosity to the village. Everyone liked him. Makarita's conduct also stoked the kind of determination that had made him champion.

Makarita was very much attracted by him and knew that she would eventually have to give in. Before she finally consented to marry him she extracted a promise that they would live in Korodamu on a piece of vacant land that belonged to her clan. All her life she had lived in the village and hated the idea of moving to the city. Even the district secondary school she had attended, and in which she taught, was within walking distance from Korodamu. Her aversion to city living was not that of people in isolated communities for whom Kuruti was another country. Korodamu was close enough to the capital to be within the ambit of its daily influence; Oilei himself, having spent so many idle months in the village, had no difficulty in accepting Makarita's condition. He had grown fond of Korodamu and had come to like rural surroundings, especially when they were conveniently close to Kuruti, but without the disadvantages of urban congestion, din and thick air. But the main reason was to be with Makarita wherever she chose to live.

Makarita's determination to live in the village was strengthened by her wish to remain close to her parents, especially in view of her father's fast-deteriorating health. She knew that he would not last much longer. Her feelings for him were more from a sense of duty than from the kind of love she had for her mother. Her generally low esteem of men developed from having to live with a semi-invalid alcoholic father, who evoked only pity in others. Although Oilei was robust, she had discerned in him the child in the man and he had a roughness that was absent from her father.

Her first real experience of Oilei's roughness was on their wedding night. Her mother had prepared the special honeymoon bed in the family house. Mere spread a brand-new starched white sheet on the pile of mats that was their bed and left beside it a bottle of fresh chicken blood she was absolutely certain they would need. No one remained in the house but the newlyweds.

Mere and just about every woman in the village were sitting under a large mango tree nearby, all set to testify to Makarita's purity. Not one soul believed in it but they observed the ritual strictly.

Inside, Makarita stripped herself naked and lay on the bed, eyes tightly closed and body quivering with trepidation, anticipating the defloration of her well-guarded maidenhead. With pent-up energy saved from an almost year-long unaccustomed chastity, Oilei went about his delicate task with the gentleness of a stampeding buffalo. But after three rounds, when Makarita was really aroused to the ecstasy of the experience and was demanding more and faster, Oilei began to flag.

Outside under the mango tree, the women could tell that the first round was over and were looking at their timepieces to measure the duration of this and subsequent intervals. At first they marvelled at Oilei's stamina, quick recuperation and staying power. But after the third round they sensed a change and from then on Makarita had the upper hand. There was one particular lady assigned to crouch under the eaves and signal to the rest the beginning and end of every round and transmit through body movement who was doing what to whom.

At dawn Oilei declared himself technically knocked out in the middle of the twelfth round. The signal was relayed and Mere tiptoed into the house, pulled the nuptial bedsheet from under them, hurried outside and let everyone see the irrefutable evidence of her daughter's recently terminated virginity. The material was splattered with much blood. A loud cheer cracked the morning stillness, followed by calls for Makarita's appearance. Eventually the door opened and Makarita stepped out, triumphantly dragging a husband who looked obviously done in.

It was only later in the day that Mere checked the bottle of chicken blood and to her utter and delighted surprise discovered it full and unused. The honeymoon night established the pattern of the couple's relationship for years to come. In long-drawn-out battles of will, Makarita gave as much as she took and often came out ahead.

After the wedding Oilei sold his interest in the taxi service and also his fifty per cent share in an old but well-kept bungalow

61

to his friend Bulbul. He moved residence to his in-laws' cramped quarters while he built with village expertise a large three-bedroom concrete dwelling with flush toilet and electricity; the most modern house in Korodamu, although it fell short of the middle-class housing standards seen in the privileged areas of Kuruti. He invested the rest of his funds in growing vegetables on his father-in-law's land, and on a small kava plantation that became his main source of income. He sold virtually all his produce for good prices to Bulbul, who, through trucking, had become an important middleman between farmers and market vendors in the city.

His father-in-law was the only surviving member of a land-holding clan in the village. As such, he had the sole control over a thirty-hectare piece of clan land, the largest in the entire district to have come through customary tenancy under the occupancy of a single individual. Upon his death, within his daughter's first year of marriage, the land passed to Makarita, which meant that effectively it was controlled by her husband. Oilei could not have been happier with the arrangement. The land he occupied was completely free from the kinds of territorial disputes that had played havoc with most attempts by indigenous Tipotans to develop commercial ventures on customarily held lands. Being thus free from traditional constraints, Oilei farmed the land unhampered and was able to earn the kind of income that placed him at the top of the village society, even if it did not provide enough to save for investment elsewhere; he had too many responsibilities in Korodamu, which looked to him as a rich uncle with limitless resources. He eventually became the chairman of the village council, and a regularly elected member of the district advisory council. He and Makarita raised a son and a daughter who were so bright that they had had no difficulty in winning their scholarships to Australian universities; one to study veterinary science and the other agricultural economics. At the time of his illness the children were still overseas and doing very well, by all reports.

As a still-famous former boxing champion, a successful peasant farmer, a pillar of Korodamu society and the sprawling district, a father of outstanding university students and a nominee for a vacant Senate seat, Oilei was at the peak of his personal achievement when he was stabbed from behind, as it were, by his very own end. Whenever he thought about it, and he had done so many times since his illness, he despaired at the unfairness of it all and vented his frustrations upon his household.

5

From Korodamu Bulbul drove toward the Rovoni Landing with
Oilei stretched out on the back seat suffering from one of his
attacks of pain in the head as well as in the arse. To reach their
destination they had to pass through Kuruti, because there was
no alternative route. The Rovoni Landing had a small jetty built
on a cleared, mangrove-forested seafront as a landing and departure point for the many small craft plying between the mainland
and the rocky island of Rovoni, sitting about a kilometre off-
shore but still in the lagoon. At low tide people walked back
and forth from the island, but since it was not so easy to
negotiate on foot and carrying loads through the mushy, mudlike
flat, most people preferred to cross on small craft at high tide.

Before the establishment of Pax Britannica in the latter half
of the nineteenth century, Rovoni was inhabited solely by a large
colony of flying foxes, which raided mainland fruit trees at night
and retreated before dawn to the safe nesting in casuarina trees
that dominated the vegetation of the island. When Christian
missionaries arrived and organised their converts into fighting
forces and imposed their new religion on the whole country,
powerful sorcerers and their families were driven from their
mainland communities to live on Rovoni and away from the
society that still feared their dangerous magic. By the second
decade of the present century the island population had been
thoroughly Christianised. Sorcerer families had ceased practising their black art and had turned themselves into first-rate
curers and healers, the largest concentration of *dottores* in the
whole of Tipota. There were reputedly at least a hundred such
practitioners living on the island.

The Rovoni Landing was generally crowded with patients and
their escorts of relatives, waiting to be ferried across to the

island. Each patient had something to take, mostly baskets of raw food and occasionally rolls of mats or tapa cloth, or live small animals and birds, for the *dottores*. As Rovoni was unsuitable for cultivation its inhabitants depended for their daily needs largely on gifts their patients brought. Their young fished in the lagoon and on the ocean side of the reefs to supplement their diet but mainly to sell their catch at the Kuruti fish market; this was the island's main source of cash income.

Bulbul did not know the name of the famous old *dottore* to whom he was taking Oilei. All *dottores* were recommended as famous even if they were known to only a handful of people and unheard of by the rest. It was sufficient for anyone to say, 'There's a well known old *dottore* in Rovoni who can cure your arse,' to persuade someone else to go there, especially if the patient had tried other famous *dottores* without avail, and was desperate. All *dottores* claimed, personally or through others, that they had treated such important people as Cabinet Ministers, high government officials, judges, lawyers, top clergymen and sports and media personalities. All claimed to have treated white people, whether or not they were important, and those whom doctors and hospitals had failed to cure.

Bulbul had obtained his sketchy information on this famous old Rovoni *dottore* from a friend in Kuruti, one Vilisoni Mateni, who had heard of him from his mate, Kailoma Jones, of Thikoiko, a town seventeen kilometres from Kuruti and on the route to the landing. Kailoma Jones had once contracted the same complaint as Oilei and was reputedly cured by the old man.

Bulbul had arranged to pick Vilisoni up at Hotel Paradesia at eleven thirty, then proceed to the Green Coconut Club at Thikoiko to fetch Kailoma, who would introduce them to the old *dottore*, who would be waiting at the landing. But just as they reached the outskirts of Kuruti, Oilei's migraine and pain in the bum had become virtually intolerable. Bulbul had to do something to give him temporary relief; they had a long way to go yet, and if he knew Vilisoni Mateni, they were more than likely to be detained at the hotel. Then he remembered his friend, the trader Ah So. He turned into a side street and took several other turns before pulling up in the parking lot of the House of the

Dragon Balm, a family firm that sold the widest range of Far Eastern spices, noodles, sweets, dried fruits and seafoods, and other unidentifiable things that went into the recipes of every Chinese restaurant in the country.

Ah So had, at least a decade back, taken up acupuncture as an adjunct to his business activities. His father and grandfather had practised it but the Tipotan-born Ah So spurned it as a primitive exercise. However, with the growing interest among non-Chinese in the practice, Ah So picked up where his father had left off. He studied his forebears' books very carefully and ordered a whole set of needles from Hong Kong. From seven till midday every morning except Sunday he conducted a clinic in a sizeable room above the company's street-level retail outlet, while his wife and niece minded the shop. His real name was Lee Ho Cheung but he had acquired the sobriquet because of his tendency for starting conversation with 'Ah So!'

Bulbul had once been treated by him for a minor but nagging pain on the knee. Two sessions with Mr Lee's needles were sufficient. Ah So handled all kinds of aches and pains, especially those of the muscles and joints. He also treated migraine, defective sight and hearing, and sinusitis, and dealt with just about any complaint brought to his attention. But his forte was treating impotence. A large number of his patients were middle-aged, middle-class men desperately seeking to maintain, regain or increase their potency. Ah So's method was simple and effective. He inserted needles around the base of the shaft, twiddling them until the lifeless member jumped to attention. Then he twiddled for a little while longer to test its staying power.

Those that lasted less than three minutes, the 'easy comers' as he called them, went through follow-up sessions until they could raise their own standards proudly. Occasionally he gave a very special client needles to take home and masturpuncture himself. For every one of his special clients he prescribed several small containers of ginseng, expensive but effective and therefore worth the investment. None of his clients ever admitted to consulting him for sexual potency; they had all kinds of convincing reasons, irrefutable because of the nature of the treatment.

Mr Lee had them all by the balls and sold them the most expensive ginseng, smiling enigmatically while he wrote the prescriptions in Chinese characters. They purchased the stuff downstairs at the shop and nowhere else because Ah So had the monopoly for importing ginseng into the country. Ah So also charged his special patients three times as much as he did the others. Once, in a moment of inebriated indiscretion, he told Bulbul that if people wanted him to make them more sinful they should bloody well pay for it. 'I'm not going to hell cheaply, no sir!'

It was assumed that Ah So's special treatment worked, for there was always a stream of notables flowing into the clinic. One journalist discovered that the best way to catch the richest, most powerful and difficult-to-find people in the country was to go to Ah So's clinic and wait. Ah So often ran out of ginseng but would have a batch flown in within a week. His supplier in Seoul was so happy that every Christmas he sent him a card, a calendar featuring the allurement of the Korean female anatomy in all its multiple manifestations, and a dozen containers of his most special ginseng, which was only for the very top-market customers in the United States, Europe and Japan. Mr Lee was a youthful seventy-seven and had just married his sixth wife, who was much less than half his age. His friends also called him Blue Beard and he could never think why.

Oilei protested heatedly when he found out what was in Bulbul's mind after he had pulled up in the Dragon Balm customers-only parking lot. He detested the idea of having needles poked into his bottom. But as he was too much in pain he relented, saying that after his experiences in the hands of Marama and Losana his arse could take just about any kind of punishment. Besides, Bulbul had assured him that the treatment was painless and there were no nurses in the clinic. As an after-thought Bulbul said, 'Acupuncture is an honourable profession. President Nixon tried it when he was in Peking. And you know what, all our top people, including the Prime Minister, don't tell anyone or you'll be deported, have been to Ah So. That's why they're always drinking ginseng for breakfast. One of them once went in there lugging a soccer ball; within ten minutes he came out with no more than a small turtle egg, no problem.'

Bulbul left Oilei moaning in the car while he went to check with Ah So, who told him that in the previous ten years he had had only a dozen patients with the pain in the arse. 'Not one ever came back for a second session, so I don't know whether I did them any good. But get Oilei here; he's worth giving it a try. I can't guarantee you anything.'

Oilei stripped, climbed on the couch with much difficulty and stretched out on his stomach.

'Ah So!' said Mr Lee. 'So it hurts a little bit, ha! And in the head too? So! We'll put a stop to them, first thing.'

He stuck a needle in each of Oilei's ankles and twiddled them. In a little over a minute he stopped.

'How's the pain? Still feeling it? No? And the migraine? Gone away too? Good, very good. You won't feel them again for a few days. Come back then and we'll do some more. You will need it then, ha! Now let's see the problem.'

He parted Oilei's buttocks and quickly closed them.

'Ah so! Not very nice to look at. You have a big problem there, ha! I have not seen anything quite like it before and I've seen quite a few arseholes in my time, ha!'

He put on a mask, had another look and poked his finger very gently around the general area. He touched something and Oilei twitched involuntarily.

'Ah so! You have a new boil on the other side of the bum. We open it up and drain out the muck. We must drain everything out and let the flesh heal. Ha! I put two needles here, not in the hole but on the side where it's been draining. There you are; it's coming out, good, so! Do you feel any pain? Good. Now I pull out the needles. Very good. Lots of pus and blood coming out. Yuk. I put some cotton wool there. It's all soaked. I drop it and put on some more. Now, I deal with the new boil on the other side. I stick two needles there. First needle, so! Second needle, so! Ha! Nothing coming out, very funny. So I stick third needle in, so! Aaaah!!! What the blurry shit! Fucking arsehole!'

Ah So cried, coughing and blowing his nose.

Oilei turned his head in time to see him fumbling for cotton wool. His face was splattered with blood and pus. Oilei could do nothing to help, for he still had the needles in his buttocks. Ah So finally found some cotton wool, cleared his eyes and nose and went stumbling across the room to a sink. He ran the tap and washed his face thoroughly, then he pulled out a bottle from the cupboard above, took a swig and rinsed his mouth. Oilei lay there helplessly looking at him as he returned and rested on the chair beside the couch. After he had caught his breath, and being a septuagenarian it took him quite some time, Ah So turned to Oilei and apologised for making the mess and losing control of himself.

'Ah so! First time it happened to me. I was completely taken by surprise. Must've touched the head when the pressure was so strong. Let's have another look.'

He rose and checked Oilei's buttocks, this time fully alert, pulled out the needles carefully and applied some cotton wool, which soaked through almost immediately.

'It's draining freely now, a lot of pus,' he applied some more. 'It's a good sign, ha! You just keep still until the flow slows down or stops altogether.'

Oilei kept still for a few minutes; the pain had gone and he was in that state of complete exhaustion he always felt following an attack. Then he fell into a deep sleep. Ah So told Bulbul to go away. 'Let him rest until he wakes himself up. It's already past closing time. Poor man. Must have gone through hell, ha! Anyway, tell him to come back in four days.'

An hour and a half later Oilei woke up to find himself under a clean sheet and on a strange couch. He did not know where he was. In a short while, when his mind was clear, he dressed and went out of the room, feeling good and fresh. Downstairs he found Bulbul talking idly with Mrs Lee.

'Well, well, here comes Sleeping Beauty. And it's bloody time too. Let's get going. Vilisoni must be pissing his pants by now. We're very late already. Thank you, Mee Chow. We'll be back in a few days.'

'Not if I can help it,' Oilei added cheerfully, gladdening Bulbul's heart. It was good to see his old friend almost back to his familiar self.

They found Vilisoni Mateni in a drunken and foul mood when they at last entered the hotel lounge bar. 'About time you bloody idiots turned up. Tell me some believable bullshit and I won't piss on your faces.'

Bulbul explained the situation in a manner that would have softened even Losana Tonoka's face. 'In that case,' Vilisoni sighed, 'let's drink to Ah So's needles. I don't care much for them myself, but let no man or beast alive say that Vilisoni Mateni's a narrow-minded son of a bitch, shit!'

They had many more than several drinks before they finally left, with Vilisoni singing all the way to the car. It was three o'clock and they were supposed to have met Kailoma at twelve.

Vilisoni went into the Green Coconut Club to fetch Kailoma Jones, who was leaning against the bar holding forth to the barman with a story he told every time he was under the weather. He laughed as he spoke but the barman looked vacantly through him. Kailoma was already past the stage of realising that he was talking only to himself.

There were no other members in the club; people would start dropping in at four thirty. He had been there since midday but by three he had forgotten why he had gone there in the first place. He was thus not upset when Vilisoni turned up late and interrupted his story.

On being reminded of what they were to do, he insisted that they had a couple before hitting the road.

'Haul yourself out and get Oilei,' he said, jabbing a finger into Vilisoni's ribs. 'I'm not leaving here until I've bought him drinks. Never met him man to man, though I went to just about every one of his fights. He was tremendous. I was a kid then. Must've been a hundred years since.' He laughed and slapped Vilisoni on the shoulder. 'Go on, man. Get him in.'

Kailoma was in the middle of the story he had been telling earlier when Bulbul interrupted.

'You had that trouble in the arse. Tell us about it.'

The barman roared, not because of the question but at the pained look on Kailoma's face as he was stopped again in the middle of his speech. He had never been able to complete that story. Every time he told it he was invariably brought down in mid-flight. No one cared about hearing the end of it, no one even cared what it was about; everyone wanted it to end for it took ever so long and Kailoma was a terrible raconteur when drunk. He never tried to tell the story when sober, nor did he ever try to tell another when drunk.

'What did you say?'

'The boil in your arse. How was it treated?'

'Ha! It was a beauty. If you've never had it, it's pointless trying to describe what it felt like. Oilei here knows all about it. I tried all kinds of medicine. None worked until I got on to Seru Draunikau, the old man we're seeing today. Oh, shit!' He looked at his watch. 'Let's go now. He'll be hopping mad at the landing. I told him we'd come before two. He normally receives patients on the island.' He nodded at Oilei. 'But he makes exception for important people.'

Before leaving they bought three cartons of beer and a bottle of gin purchased by Oilei for the old man. Seru loved nothing more than gin, Kailoma said, and also explained that a reason for the old man receiving them at the landing was the prohibition on storing and consumption of alcohol on the island, a stricture that had forced the inhabitants to use the shed at the landing as an evening drinking place, which was thus also patronised by men from nearby villages. Walled on three sides, it had been built for no economic reason by the Tipota Port Authority during a general election campaign. Its reputation for violence was well known and recently, after two men were fatally stabbed with broken beer bottles, the police had been raiding it regularly, often sneaking in from the sea in patrol boats with their engines cut.

Seru Draunikau was one of the very few well-educated and well-travelled old men in the country. He was such a promising student at school that when one of his missionary teachers returned home to Britain he took Seru with him to further his education. Seru lived in London for nearly a dozen years, and after completing his university education he returned home and taught at his old mission school, rising to the post of deputy principal when the Second World War broke out. Using his London connections, Seru found his way back to England, joined the

71

Army and saw action in North Africa and Europe. At his demobilisation he did what very few ex-servicemen did: he rejected the modern world and returned to his native island of Rovoni to immerse himself in things traditional. But he could not give up the habit of drinking alcohol that he had acquired during his army career. He also kept a shortwave radio and, by tuning mainly to the BBC and the Voice of America, kept abreast of current world events, which only strengthened his resolve to maintain his distance from developments occurring around him. It was said of him that as he grew older he became increasingly odd in his behaviour.

It was well after five when Bulbul pulled up at the landing. They had expected to find the old man hopping mad but he was not. He was sitting on the ground, propped against the shed, holding a newly opened bottle of gin with an empty one lying in front of him. Nearby sat his twelve-year-old grandson, Varani, nursing a pair of trussed chickens. Otherwise the landing was deserted.

Seru Draunikau was the leading Rovoni specialist in all diseases found between the waist and the knees and was considered the top Tipotan bum *dottore*. His reputation was not publicly trumpeted, for his clients preferred to spread it only to fellow sufferers. Neither he nor they wanted the public at large to know what they were doing, especially when some of the most powerful men in the country were involved.

'Glad you came,' Seru said as he shook hands with Oilei. 'See this bottle? Came from a Cabinet Minister. That empty one over there? From a big shot Opposition fella. Worst arseholes I've ever seen. The chooks are from the president of the TTUC. Should've seen his; looked like an abandoned factory furnace.' He pulled out a pocket Bible. 'With the compliments of the Archbishop. Mean, miserly bum. Fancy giving something like this to a starving man! Here, you have it,' he called out, tossing the book to Bulbul. 'If you can't read it, curry it!' The old man laughed. 'Now sit down and have a drink before we fix you up.'

It was well after dark when Oilei suggested that perhaps it was time to do something about his problem. Seru nodded and rose, indicating to the patient to follow him. They went to the sea side of the shed, where Oilei pulled his pants down and bent forward. The old man shone a torch and examined his buttocks very closely since his eyesight was failing. Oilei could feel him breathing into his arse.

'Phew! That's awful. It definitely calls for a steaming treatment. I . . .'

*'Freeze!!! Don't move, you disgusting poofters!!!'* the loudspeaker blared.

A blazing, blinding searchlight suddenly illuminated the spot where Oilei and Seru were standing. The patrol boat had sneaked in from the sea, seen the torchlight trained on someone's bottom and gone *presto* into action.

After a momentary paralysis Oilei bellowed, 'Police!! Run!! Into the car for Chrissake!! Run!!'

For a group of drunks, they sped as if they were on an Olympic track. Seru swooped up his gin, Varani his squawking chooks, the others their remaining beer and bolted.

'Your grandfather's a fucking pervert!!'

'Should've seen his arse lit up!! Bloody full moon!!'

'Got his nose so close he might as well've kissed my arse!!!'

They drove into a side road five kilometres away and pulled up laughing their heads off – except Varani, who dared not say anything on account of his grandfather's presence.

For the first time in months Oilei was enjoying himself so thoroughly that he stopped worrying about his problem. Ah So's needles had done their job wonderfully. But he reminded himself that it was only temporary and he must go back for more needles. He pushed those thoughts away and joined in the revelry.

When they had drunk everything in sight Bulbul drove them back to the landing, checking first that the coast was clear before pulling up. They all piled out and Seru disappeared into the mangroves with Varani to fetch the medicine. Kailoma was still far from halfway into his old story when grandfather and grandson emerged from the forest carrying small branches with the leaves still on them. Damn! he muttered to himself and quietly sulked.

Seru told Oilei that there were sufficient leaves there for a

73

five-day steaming treatment. 'Pick them off when you get home; leave them in a fridge and take out only what you need. Boil some water and pour it into a container over which you squat naked. Cover yourself and the hot water with a blanket to retain the steam. When it gets too hot, and you will certainly feel it, get up and cool yourself before squatting again. Don't try to brave it out or you'll cook your balls.

'Do it twice a day. By the third day you'll feel a lot better; by the fifth your problem should be over completely. Don't forget that I treated those nobs today. You're in good company.'

Oilei thanked the old man profusely and went over to Varani to give him the bottle of gin he had kept in the car.

'It's for your grandfather,' he said and patted his head.

The four of them piled into the car and drove off. Just before they left, Oilei overheard Seru say, 'Go bury it in the hiding place.'

They dropped Kailoma Jones off at Thikoiko, Vilisoni at his home in Kuruti, and spent the night at Bulbul's. They woke up in the afternoon of the following day, had a light meal and drove on to Korodamu.

Makarita was furious but was quickly pacified by Bulbul's deft explanation. She roared when she heard of the police raid, and teased Oilei about it. To her surprise her husband took the ribbing good-naturedly. She had expected him to explode as he had done for so long, but it was obvious that something good had happened the previous day.

She went whistling into the kitchen to put on the kettle while Oilei looked for a suitable container. He decided on an empty half-gallon Milo tin, but since he found it difficult to squat with legs wide apart while maintaining a tense position above the tin, he had to find a more comfortable way of doing it. As he passed by the toilet a thought flashed across his mind; he went in and placed the tin in the toilet bowl. It fitted in snugly with the top reaching just below the seat. He sat and discovered that the bowl was well covered by his body so there was no need for a blanket to retain the steam.

When the water boiled Oilei poured it into the tin, tossed in two handfuls of leaves and sat over it. The heat became unbear-

74

able so he rose to cool himself, then sat down again. He repeated this several times.

Makarita and Bulbul were at the dining table talking and drinking tea when they heard the shriek, 'Oh, shit!! Rita!! Rita!!'

'Here we go again,' Makarita muttered as she rose, followed by Bulbul. They found Oilei bending arse over, violently scratching his groin.

'What's the matter?' Makarita asked, barely suppressing her laughter.

'Scratch me, Rita. The itch's killing me. Scratch!!!'

'Scratch your what?' she broke up.

'Scratch my arse, you stupid bitch!! Get to!!!'

'Scratch your own bloody . . .'

She never finished, for Oilei straightened up with a mighty punch that glanced off her temple but still had sufficient impact to knock her out cold.

As Makarita fell backward into the lounge Oilei leapt on her, reaching for the throat. Bulbul saw what was about to happen, grabbed the nearest chair, held it aloft and crashed it on Oilei's head. He sank on Makarita's inert body.

Bulbul dragged Oilei off, turned him over on his back, checked his breathing, his eyes, and his head where a large lump was forming. He went into the bedroom, pulled out a sheet and spread it over Oilei's naked body. Then he worked on Makarita in a similar manner, except that being fully dressed, she needed only her clothing straightened out. From his boxing-ring experience he knew that they would come off well but with a little headache to endure for a while.

Bulbul sat on the divan mulling over what had just happened. Oilei had never before hit Makarita, that he knew. And he could not recall any time since his boxing days when Oilei had punched anyone else. He would roar and threaten, but that was all. Since the previous day Oilei had been particularly cheerful. Something must have snapped. He vividly recalled his face when he demanded of Makarita to scratch him. It was that of a crazed beast. The itch's killing me, he had said. That's it, the treatment, something in it had caused the itch, the demand for scratching, the crazed animal look, the savage attack.

75

He went over and checked Oilei's groin and buttocks. Angry welts and even blisters were forming. He went to the kitchen and emptied the dregs from the teapot into a bowl, added a teaspoon of salt, went outside, picked a lemon and squeezed it in. He stirred the mixture thoroughly as he returned to the lounge and then rubbed it on Oilei's private parts and buttocks. Returning the rest to the kitchen, he went back to the divan and waited.

Makarita stirred and Bulbul went over to help her up. She shook him off angrily, sat still for a while, rose gingerly to her feet, looked at Bulbul, and then at Oilei with utmost loathing.

'You can have him. I'm leaving and will never return.' She meant every word of it.

Close to an hour later, Oilei opened his eyes. Bulbul was standing at the door ready to move swiftly if necessary. He had turned the car around and run the engine, keeping it ready for a quick getaway. Constable Butako, who had come to investigate after Makarita's complaint, stood by outside, also ready for a quick retreat should the big man become violent.

Oilei sat up shaking his head, looking utterly confused.

'What happened?' he asked Bulbul.

The crazed look had gone. Bulbul gave the prearranged signal to Butako to switch off the car engine. He sighed with relief, went to Oilei, touched him briefly and sat down beside him. He told him all that had happened and of his suspicion of the medicine. Oilei could not remember anything. The itch had disappeared, although he felt raw down below.

'I'm going to Rovoni to have it out with the old man. He has a lot to answer for. Rita could have died and it'd have been his fault,' Bulbul said.

'Yes. Poor Rita. Poor me. I don't know what to do. Come straight back after you've seen him, will you. I need you. I guess Rita does too. I can't believe that I actually hit her. I must have gone completely off my head. It'll serve me right if she never comes back.'

'We'll see about that later,' Bulbul said grimly as he left.

The sun was sinking when the old man approached the jetty in a small dinghy propelled by a two-horsepower Seagull outboard motor. Seagull motors were the most popular among the poor; they were easy on petrol and maintenance, and with them, anyone could become an expert mechanic. On any given day several craft would be seen drifting aimlessly in the lagoon with broken-down Seagull motors. Their handlers invariably got them going again, however long it took. Seru moored his dinghy to the jetty, stepped out and disappeared into the mangroves. He came out shortly clutching a bottle of gin, trudged across to the shed and sat down leaning against it. He was taking his second swig from the bottle when Bulbul walked up and flung a branch at him.

'What's that in aid of?' Seru Draunikau demanded, surprised at Bulbul's rudeness.

'That's what you gave Oilei last night. Look at it carefully and tell me what it is.'

Seru took time examining the leaves closely, mounting horror written clearly on his face. When satisfied that it was what he suspected it to be, he put the branch carefully aside, looked up at Bulbul and said, 'Merciful Lord. Did I actually give him that?' He took a long swig from the bottle, his hands shaking. 'Is he all right? What of the people in the village? Was anyone hurt?'

'He was all right when I left, but he nearly killed his own wife, thanks to you. Tell me about the plant,' Bulbul demanded, unaffected by the old man's obvious distress.

Seru took another long swig, screwed the bottle top back on, put it down between his outstretched legs and told the story of the plant.

In the olden days before Christianity and colonialism proscribed tribal warfare, some chiefs rubbed their warriors' bodies with the kautambu leaves just before confronting their enemies. The leaves made the warriors so itchy that they were transformed into bloodthirsty beasts and remorseless killers. If there were no enemies and the itch was on, the warriors would turn on their own people, even their closest relatives, and slaughter them. Kautambu was used with the greatest of precautions. Fortunately, however, the plant was extremely rare and could not be cultivated. It did not grow in colonies; every kautambu that had ever been found was alone, far away from others already

77

discovered. Their life span after discovery was extremely short, no longer than a few months. How they grew was an unresolved mystery.

Chiefs employed special people, most of whom were sorcerers, to search for the plant almost on a full-time basis. On the very rare occasions when the plant was found, the side that used it, however weak it might normally have been, smashed through its enemies slaughtering everyone on sight. The effect of the itch lasted roughly an hour but this period was sufficient to allow for much destruction.

Seru averred that when he was a child he usually went with his grandfather looking for medicinal plants. On one occasion, the minute details of which remained vivid in his memory, the grandfather came upon a kautambu. Since Seru had seen it too the grandfather explained what it was and what it could do. Grandfather spent the rest of that day and the following piling up dry wood around the plant until it was totally covered. After he had ascertained that there was more than enough needed for the job, he lit the bonfire.

The problem with kautambu, Seru said, was that it looked almost like kambawangga, the plant he normally used for the arse-steaming treatment. Only a well-trained eye could tell the difference. Seru was probably the only living human being to have seen a kautambu.

'I shall most probably spend the rest of my days looking for kautambu and destroying them,' and he looked Bulbul in the eye. 'It's the most dangerous plant there is. I'm very, very sorry for what happened to Oilei and Makarita.'

'Then show your regret in the proper manner,' Bulbul suggested.

'Certainly. I'll come to Korodamu tomorrow or the day after at the latest.'

Oilei was alone in the house feeling utterly miserable when he heard the car pull up outside. There was a knock and Bulbul walked in followed by Makarita and Mere. On his return from the landing Bulbul had driven straight to Mere's and told them the whole story and of the old man's readiness to make amends. He was so consummate at recounting it that Mere sobbed and

Makarita cried, and before they realised what was happening they were already in the car heading home.

'It's the first time you've come back after sunset,' Oilei cracked.

'What do you expect after hitting me like that?' Makarita grieved.

'You're lucky to be still alive.'

'You're lucky I'm back, itchy arse,' Makarita retorted, heading straight to her room.

6

After Bulbul had left him, Seru sat immobile for a long time thinking about what had happened and what he must do. He did not once take another swig from the bottle. He was deeply concerned with what might happen to his practice, for his family's livelihood depended largely on it. If word spread widely that because of his drunkenness he had almost brought disaster upon a national hero, they too would suffer. He knew all too well that when stories spread they grew in all dimensions and became utterly distorted.

He must see Oilei as soon as possible and get his arse fixed up. He alone must do it if his reputation were to be saved. The idea of continuing with steaming was out. Oilei would reject it outright and no one would blame him. He must be persuaded, if necessary compelled, to take from him treatment of another kind.

Seru rose, went to the edge of the jetty and smashed the bottle. He threw its neck as far out into the water as he could. Crossing the passage back home, he vowed never again to touch another drop of liquor.

In bed that night he dreamt a dream that clarified in his mind the basic causes of human illness in general, and the true nature of Oilei's problem in particular. More than that, he was convinced that he had had a vision and had been appointed by the Unseen to carry out a mission that would revolutionise the whole practice of medicine. Oilei had been appointed by the same agency to be the first beneficiary of the new approach.

Seru was woken by his dream and stayed up for the rest of the night, transported by the revelation. What he would do from then on would no longer bear much relationship to his personal life or the welfare of his family. Henceforth he had to work for the benefit of all human beings, wherever they might be. He was a new man, a prophet.

Just before dawn and with his drowsy wife's help, he selected five of the finest mats they had stacked on the rafters. He ordered his son to catch the biggest pig in the pen, and to prepare a large bundle of kava. Then he had his entire family accompany him to Korodamu. They left the island early to catch the seven o'clock bus to Kuruti. At the landing Seru sent Varani on an errand into the mangroves while he and his son went into the bush behind. They returned shortly with two plastic shopping bags, each containing a different kind of leaves. Varani had already come back with seven bottles of gin, all that there was in the cache. Hardly a word passed between them, for Seru appeared to be different, possessing something the others had never before detected in him. He had an aura of authority, of a man who had seen a mystery and had solved it.

Oilei was relaxing on the divan talking with Makarita and Mere when the visitors from Rovoni appeared. They had disembarked some distance away, disrobed and wrapped tapa cloth around themselves, donned tiaras of Tahitian chestnut leaves and then proceeded slowly to Oilei's house, chanting an ancient tune about being washed up on a strange shore. The men carried their burden on their shoulders, the women bore the mats on their heads.

Mere and Makarita shifted all the furniture to the spare bedroom and brought in a large bowl, a bucket of water and a packet of pounded kava, which they placed at the far end of the lounge. There they sat down slightly behind Oilei, facing the entrance. Seru and his family entered bearing the gifts and placed them in the middle of the lounge. His son took the kava they had brought and placed it in front of Oilei, then returned to the other end of the room where his family sat. Oilei put a hand on the kava and left it there until everyone had registered his action.

Seru spoke first with the formality, self-abasement and praise of others that went with ceremonial presentations. He thanked Oilei for honouring him and his poor, humble family by receiving them in the beautiful house only a man of wealth and renown could have built.

'Rovoni, as everyone in the Pacific knows, is rocky and infer-
tile,' Seru continued. 'Its destitute people are unable to grow
or make anything in the quality and quantity that you, who live
on more favourable soils, can produce without any difficulty.
But whatever little that we can produce we do with loving care,
as you can see in the happy, contented face of this tiny piglet
that I have dared to present to you, Oilei Bomboki, who are
accustomed to receiving only great tusked boars and bulls as
a matter of course. I beg you most humbly to accept this half
a cent worth of lowly things that we have brought.

'I come to you with a heavy heart. The wrong that I have done
to you came solely from the carelessness and stupidity of old
men in their declining years. I beg you therefore to forgive me
and spare the few days I have left before I heed the trumpet
call that will summon me to Jehovah or to the other one, as the
case may be.

'Should you forgive and spare my miserable life, I will do all
there is in my power to remove from your body the pain Jehovah
in his mysterious ways has visited upon you. I offer you, sir,
the best that my profession can render. I, more than anyone,
know that, after your near tragic experience, you would consider my suggestion an effrontery. And I would more than
deserve it if you throw me out or beat me up. But, like the
prophet Daniel who went, as instructed by Jehovah, into the
lion's den to remove the thorn from the beast's paw, I'm risking
my limbs and life, and indeed those of my family, by entering
your domain, as instructed by the Holy Saviour, to remove the
thorn from your, er, organ. This is my humble submission and
I beg you to give it the gravest and most favourable con-
sideration.'

Oilei was very angry and would have exploded had custom
not demanded that he must, in the ritual situation, behave with
decorum and due ceremony. He had accepted the kava that was
in front of him and had instructed his wife to prepare kava for
the visitors. In the presence of the two kava and of the much
larger than normal atonement presentation in the middle of his
lounge, he could not and must not show any sign of anger. What
made Oilei even more inwardly furious was the way the old man

82

had put him in a corner from which he could not escape without considerable loss of face. He could not barefacedly reject an offer nor refuse a request, especially when they were for his own benefit. To do so would bring him dishonour. Without the kava and the presentation Oilei would have had no compunction in throwing Seru and his family out of his house. He thus sat silently and absolutely still for several minutes before responding. He must deal with the old man's speech point by point and phrase his words in such a manner as to extricate himself from Seru's clutch without offending the guests.

When he spoke, it was with the utmost humility and courtesy. He thanked Seru and his family for honouring his humble abode with their very presence. They had brought with them the fresh and aromatic winds that, since creation, had swept the shores of their beautiful and justly famous island. 'I am but a poor ignorant farmer who dares not compare himself with the eminent *dottores* of Rovoni, the greatest healing centre in the whole South Pacific. The health and happiness of all the people of our beloved Tipota depend almost entirely on your vast knowledge of medicine and on the skills that line the palms of your hands.

'What you have given me may be worth only half a cent to people like those of your island, because you earn so much with your brains and delicately skilled hands that whatever piece of gold you choose to throw into pigsties, as is mentioned in the Holy Book, means nothing to you. But I, the poor ignorant farmer, will forever cherish the great treasure you have so generously given. This huge animal may be only a piglet to you because pigs in Rovoni are born huge. We have always marvelled at how enormous your pigs grow, larger than elephants. In all my life I've never received anything like what you have just honoured me with. I refer not to the great animal and mats and kava but to something else. No one, not even my wealthiest friend, has ever given me more than two bottles of spirits. Being so poor, I have never been able to buy more than one bottle for myself let alone for anyone else. Seven bottles of gin from one person is a fabulous gift, which only a Rovoni could give.

'Seru Draunikau, you could have chosen eight or more or six or less bottles of gin but being a great Rovoni intellectual, you have chosen to give me seven. Seven, the most magical of numbers, is impregnated with great significance and history as old as the universe. In seven days Jehovah created the solar system and the galaxy. Seven apostles finally made it into Heaven without dying first. King Solomon of the Israelites had no less than seven wives and many more than seven hundred. It's in the Book. Seven also stands for the greatest movies ever made in Hollywood: *The Magnificent Seven*, *Seven Brides for the Seven Brothers*, *The Seven Merry Wives of Windsor*, *The Seven Dwarfs on the Sleeping Beauty* and *The Seven Deadly Sins*. I have been most honoured and blessed today with the Seven Gins from Seru, the most unique and splendid gift ever presented in the entire history of Tipota.

'You asked me to forgive you. Who am I to forgive anyone? The Holy Book says that forgiveness is the Lord's prerogative. I have nothing in my mind but the fondest and sweetest of memories of my too-brief friendship with you. Two days ago you gave me the most enjoyable evening I'd had for a long, long time. And the gift you have just presented is worth ten times the experience that I had yesterday, although I would not voluntarily go through it again. If you have already made your peace with the Lord then that is more than I have longed for. In fact I prayed almost all last night to the Heavenly Father to take good care of you, my friend and brother in Christ.

'Finally, I would like to say something about any further treatment of my problem. This is a matter to be decided upon between you, me and the Lord. I'm indeed honoured to have been likened to a magnificent lion with a thorn in his paw. And I can understand why the Good Lord would send his prophet Daniel into a lion's den. Lions and lionesses are the most awe-inspiring beasts in the Lord's creation, and the great English poet William Bligh, whose work I read in my school days, wrote the greatest animal poem ever composed, praising the magnificent lion burning bright in the middle of the night. Yes, the Lord would indeed send a prophet to save a lion; but I doubt very much that the same Lord would despatch a prophet into a rathole to save a useless mouse, especially when the Lord himself had inflicted boils on the said rodent's, er, body. I am, in other words and in short, not worthy of any further medical attention by you or the Holy Saviour. The last thing I want is to make any further impositions on your divinely endowed skills and talents. You must, at your advanced age, be very tired by your remarkable exertions today. May I suggest therefore that you forget everything and have a good rest, after which you must have some refreshments before returning to your famed and fair island.'

To this unmistakable rejection of his offer, Seru very gently announced, 'As I have put it to you, the Lord Jehovah has sent me into the lion's den to remove the thorn from the magnificent beast's magnificent paw. As a devout Christian I must obey the Almighty, even though the lion may very well tear me up for his dinner. I have entered the lion's den, and if it be the Lord's will, then whatever remains of me may be taken home by my family to be buried next to my revered father and beloved mother.'

Oilei sat there staring at Seru incredulously, realising that he had been outmanoeuvred by a foxy old man. There was nothing else he could do but submit himself once more to his ministration.

'In that case then, let the Lord's will be done. But my good friend, I implore you most earnestly to execute the divine order with utmost care and precision, for if anything goes amiss this time, I have only the vaguest notion of what the Heavenly Father will do to you through his humble servant, namely me. Makarita, please serve the kava,' Oilei said very calmly, bowing courteously to Seru in the way he always did to his boxing opponents just before he rose to demolish them.

When the first round of kava had been served and the formality of the occasion had thereby ended, the visitors changed into their normal clothes and sat relaxed, or more correctly, trying to be at ease with their hosts around the kava bowl. But the atmosphere was too palpably tense to allow for complete relaxation. In a little while the women left for the kitchen to prepare lunch, leaving the men to talk among themselves. Their conversation drifted inevitably to what was uppermost in their minds, the treatment. It was then that Seru revealed as a preface to what was to come his amazing dream of the human body and the creatures that lived in it.

In his vision Seru saw the human body as a world in itself, a world inhabited by human-like creatures, the tuktuks, who organised themselves into tribes occupying territories located only in those parts of the body that contained organs and members, the most populous being lands in the lower erogenous regions. The arms and the legs were completely uninhabited and were visited only occasionally by a few intrepid hunters.

Tuktuk territories were grouped into upper and lower zones. Uppertuk tribes were those that occupied territories above the solar plexus, the Lowertuk tribes being those that lived from the abdomen down. Within each zone tribes were ranked according to their relative locations, above or below each other, the highest being those in the brain territories, the lowest those tuktuks who lived in the arse and the genitals.

It was the brain tribes who invented the ranking system, claiming that since they were the only ones who could see, hear and smell things outside their body-world because of their commanding proximity to its major apertures, and that since they lived in the loftiest territories, far above the muck in the abdomen and the filth in the anal region, they were the best and cleanest tuktuks of all. They also believed that they were the cleverest since they had the good sense to live in the best part of the body-world. Uppertuks said that the worst, nastiest, dirtiest, smelliest, vilest and generally the most beastly tuktuks were those who occupied the largely swampy territories of the arse. The most degenerate, horny, porno-brained, disgustingly obscene, perverted and generally the most licentiously abandoned and loathsome were tuktuks who lived in the genital region.

Tuktuks subsisted on hunting ninongs, moose-like creatures that fed upon germs. They hunted with bows and arrows, spears and boomerangs. Because ninongs lived in different environments and fed upon different types of germs, they varied greatly in kind, size, taste and nutritional composition. The largest, tastiest, most nutritious and therefore the most desired and prized were called nambawan ninongs, found only in the genital and anal territories. These heavenly creatures fed upon a special type of germ carried around by crab lice that inhabited the nethermost regions and nowhere else. It was natural therefore that anal and genital tuktuks called their parts of the body-world the Happy Hunting Grounds.

From the milk of the nambawan ninong was made a unique kind of cheese known as liebfraufromage, which had the aroma of the Red Rose of Sodom and the combined taste of twenty species of the Forbidden Fruit. Since this cheese was matured only by being buried for ten years in anal swamps, it was the exclusive product of the arse dwellers. Tuktuks were known to have sold their entire families down the drain for a single bite of the liebfraufromage.

Since tuktuks lived entirely on ninongs and ninong dairy products, it was absolutely necessary that they trade with each other in order to vary their diet and broaden their nutritional bases. The ninong trade was conducted and controlled by tribes in the brain region who had convinced all others of their superior organisational ability and business honesty. The main trade route to and from the brain region was the spinal cord, while the nerves served as roads that branched out to the rest of the body-world. Groups of ninong traders and their long lines of carriers were always tracking from one territory to another, buying and selling. There was fierce competition among these traders for the body-world distribution of liebfraufromage and nambawan ninongs.

Between the Uppertuks of the brain region and the Lowertuks of the anal and genital territories, there was little love lost. Much of their mutual animosity arose from the Uppertuk resentment of the fact that the things they wanted most were available only in the lowest regions. To obtain these products they had to go to those areas that to them were extremely unhealthy, filthy and disgusting, and deal with tribes they considered far beneath them in intelligence and in physical and moral cleanliness. Through their familiarity with these lowest regions the brain Uppertuks had amassed a corpus of epithets that they freely hurled at Lowertuks, words directly related to the perceived characteristics of their environments. Uppertuks called Lowertuks arseholes, arselickers, buggers, bums, bullshitters, cocksuckers, cunts, fart faces, fuckwits, fucking this, fucking that, greedy guts, shitheads, turds, wankers and other luridly offensive expressions. They characterised the mental and moral capacities of Lowertuks as piss weak and shit awful and their achievements as cockups. Lowertuk tattooists, cave painters, bone carvers, nose-flute players, chanters and rain dancers were referred to as arty farty bullshit artists and poofters. In the department of invective, Lowertuks were at a distinct disadvantage. They could not use the words Uppertuks had invented for them because that would only demean their surroundings, of which they were extremely fond and proud. And since not one of them had ever been to the brain lands they knew next to nothing about life in the lofty region. All they could say of the Uppertuks were that they were dunderheads, thickheads, dummkopf, dumdum, bird-brained, nitwit, numbskull, scatter-brained, stupid, boofy, gormless, and other similarly inoffensive expressions.

Peace, stability and prosperity prevailed in the body-world as long as ninongs abounded in every territory, each tribe limited its hunting to its own domain, no one tried to monopolise or in any way interfere wth the ninong trade, and tuktuks confined their conflicts to exchanges of invective.

'Human beings are healthy only as long as the tuktuks inside them live in relative peace,' Seru said. 'But since there is no such thing as a perfect body-world, tuktuks are always in strife. Sometimes they confine their conflicts within a single territory, at times two or more regions are involved, and every now and then the whole body-world is at war. All diseases and illnesses in the human body and mind are caused by the messy tribal and intertribal relationships among the tuktuks.

'Oilei, your bottom's in a mess and your head's in turmoil because of long-drawn-out struggles between the arse and the brain tuktuks and among the brain dwellers themselves.'

Many years before Oilei was stricken, Seru said, a ninong trading expedition headed by Bongotuk, chieftain of the smallest brain tribe, went to the anal region to get as many of the nambawan ninongs and as much liebfraufromage as he could for the initiation feast of his eldest daughter. While en route Bongotuk left the track on the only hill inside the region to attend to a call of nature. As he stepped a little distance into the bush he found a cave, the small mouth of which hid a huge natural chamber in which were stacked mounds of tuktuk skeletons. Bongotuk knew instantly that he had stumbled into the secret burial place of the anal tuktuks, the most sacred of their sacred grounds, which, until then, no outside tuktuk had ever seen. Being an Uppertuk who held the utmost contempt for Lowertuks, Bongotuk defecated in the cave without qualm. While squatting he picked up a shining round object and started bouncing it. He noticed that the cave was also piled high with similar objects and said to himself, 'I must take some for my little children.' He stuffed many balls into his shoulder bag and left.

When the expedition returned home, Bongotuk bounced one ball in front of his children. As it bounced around it fell into the fireplace and exploded loudly, shattering a potful of ninongs. Bongotuk was amazed. He threw in another ball, which exploded with a terrific bang. Then he placed a trussed-up ninong near the fire and banged another ball, which killed the creature instantly. He thought for a while and, being a brainy tuktuk, searched for a strip of highly inflammable material, which he attached to another ball, lit it and tossed the lot into the air. It went off and blew to pieces a large germ flying by.

Being a cruel and unscrupulous leader, Bongotuk saw in the balls the means to attain his long-held ambition to become the paramount chief of all the brain tribes and therefore control the entire ninong and liebfraufromage trade. Accordingly he sent his three sons and trusted minions secretly to the cave to fetch a large supply of balls, which he used to impose his dominance over all the hitherto-independent brain tribes and united them under a single rule for the first time ever. He had also despatched a strong force of warriors to take possession of the cave and prevent anyone else from gaining access.

The anal tuktuks protested vehemently against the desecration of their sacred ground. When these protests fell on deaf ears they mounted a series of attacks on the intruders, who easily repelled them with their explosives, killing a great number. Those who survived were hounded and slaughtered mercilessly, and their families massacred. In time Bongotuk subjugated the anal and genital tuktuks, forced them into breeding nambawan ninongs and manufacturing more liebfraufromage, levying a seventy per cent tax in kind on all that they produced. Bongotuk also subjugated all the other tribes of the Lowertuk territories and was set on conquering the rest of the body-world. At the home front, Bongotuk's tribe had formed the ruling class of the new paramountcy and had reduced all the other tribes to the rank of carriers in the ninong trade. Bongotuk was hated both at home and abroad.

'Almost a year ago, just before you started feeling the pain in your arse,' Seru addressed Oilei, 'the anal tuktuks, instigated by their intolerable oppression and the continued desecration of their most sacred ground, rose in an open rebellion against their oppressors. From the beginning they have used guerrilla tactics because their weapons cannot match those of Bongotuk's forces. They normally ambush Bongotuk's troops and retreat quickly into the deepest and densest swamps, where enemy warriors would not go on account of the filth and the stench. Using bows to fire explosive missiles, Uppertuks are bombarding these swamps, thus giving you the nasty pain in the arse.

'Even more recently the brain tuktuks from the oppressed tribes have taken advantage of the diversion caused by the Lowertuk rebellion to rise and fight for their own liberation. They are set on overthrowing the ruling class. Bongotuk's warriors are bombarding the rebels, causing the nasty migraine that has doubled your suffering.

'The point is that there are two full-scale rebellions in your body-world. There's civil war in your brain and a Lowertuk guerrilla campaign against foreign domination. Your pains will persist as long as these conflicts remain unresolved. You will have even more pain if the other Lowertuk tribal territories rise against Bongotuk.'

'That's the most fantastic thing I've ever heard, Seru,' Oilei marvelled. 'The rebellions sound exactly like what you hear from the BBC news service every day.'

'You are at liberty to make any comparisons or draw any parallels you like, but I'm only interested in your complaints. You see, we must help the anal tuktuks drive away their invaders, and must also assist the other tuktuk tribes in the brain to overthrow the same oppressors.

In short, my recommendation is that we help the freedom fighters of the two connected revolutions, and liberate all oppressed tuktuks. Once we get rid of Bongotuk's hordes from your arse and brain, his henchmen and lackeys in the other territories will be easily swept away. Only when this is done will your pains disappear.'

Everyone in the group was profoundly impressed by Seru's revelation. They had never heard anything like it before. For long minutes they sat absolutely still, staring in awed wonderment at the old *dottore*, who appeared to each of them the very image of the Holy Physician's father. At long last it was Oilei who broke the spell.

'Pardon me, Seru, why didn't the other tuktuks look for their own explosives in other caves?'

'All the explosives in your body-world are found only in the one anal cave,' Seru explained. 'The anal tuktuks always take their dying relatives to the cave and leave them there to die among the remains of their ancestors. Just before they expire, they fart out all the methane gas in their bodies. The atmosphere in the cave is saturated with a certain type of gas found nowhere else. When each fart comes out and meets the unique atmosphere of the cave, it curls up and solidifies into a shiny, bouncing ball, which explodes when it touches anything hot. I hope that this explanation satisfies you. Now let's get back to your problem.

'You will have a series of smoking treatments of your bottom and head. It's new and untried and was only revealed to me last night. There are two types of leaves you will use as your revolutionary weapons. One is for gassing those Uppertuk invaders in your arse. The other is for the overthrow of the Bongotuk ruling tribe in your brain,' Seru paused to give Oilei a bag. 'That contains leaves that you put in a slow smouldering fire over which you expose your bottom. I'll show you later how it's done.

91

You will do it six times, which should be sufficient to get rid of every Uppertuk intruder down there.'

Seru gave Oilei the other bag.

'Roll some leaves in that bag in a sheet of dry banana leaf to make a cigar. Light and sniff the cigar while you're smoking your behind. That should destroy Bongotuk and all his gang living luxuriously in your brain.

'I'll keep you company for the first treatment, although my bottom isn't in any way whatsoever diseased, unlike some people I know. We'll begin when you're ready. We will need two strong wooden boxes, some dry coconut husks and banana leaves, and a place where we will have complete privacy.

'Before we start, let me tell you that this new treatment has the potential to benefit human beings everywhere. I'm certain that it will revolutionise medical science as Isaac Newton's work revolutionised physics. The discovery of tuktuks will most probably rank above Louis Pasteur's discovery of germs. Think about it.'

Oilei led Seru to an old and rather dilapidated but dry backyard shed with a concrete floor that he used as a packing and storage facility for his kava and other farm produce. Near the entrance stood a carpenter's bench on top of which was a box of tools. The shed was otherwise empty except for a few old sacks, wooden packing boxes strewn on the floor, and Oilei's farming implements leaning against a corner wall. He tidied up the floor and selected the two largest and sturdiest boxes. In the bottom boards in each he opened a square hole large enough to accommodate not too uncomfortably one human bottom. He placed the boxes on the ground and sat on each of them in turn; they held firm. He went out and returned with an armful of dry coconut husks and banana leaf. They had all they needed for the job.

Seru instructed Oilei on exactly what to do and excused himself to attend to an urgent call of nature. Everything was ready on his return. Two small fires were smouldering slowly on the middle of the floor, about two metres apart. Oilei had already tossed in some green leaves and there was a fair amount of rising smoke but not enough to befog the shed. Oilei had also rolled two six-inch cigars, one of which he offered Seru, who closed his eyes and said a brief prayer before signalling Oilei to begin. They stripped themselves naked, took a box each, stood them over the fires and sat down facing each other. Then they lit the cigars and held them as close to their noses as they comfortably could, and sniffed.

After about ten minutes Seru realised that he could not get any more smoke up through his nostrils, although the cigar was still well alive. He tried again before he felt something odd, very odd indeed, something he had never before experienced. He had ceased to breathe, no air moved in or out of his nose or mouth. He tried again but nothing happened. He did not panic, for he was not running out of breath. His lungs and heart seemed to function as they always did, and his pulse rate was normal. Then he realised with horror what had happened. He looked sharply at Oilei, who was staring at him almost completely stunned.

'Are you having the same experience I'm having?' Seru asked in a peculiar voice.

'You mean you're also breathing through your arse?' Oilei croaked back.

Before Seru could respond Oilei farted – through his nose. And Seru, to his own amazement, farted right back, also through his nose.

'Bloody hell!'

'Oh, shit!'

Seru was clumsily unrolling his cigar when he heard Oilei croaking like a dying Mafia godfather saying his last words.

'It's a miracle!' Oilei began giggling like a moron, but without making a sound.

'Miracle my arse!' Seru croaked angrily and almost inaudibly back. 'You've made the cigars with the wrong leaves, you stupid arsehole!'

He reached to the ground and picked up the plastic bag from which Oilei had taken the leaves for the fire. They were also wrong.

Seru rose, switched the bags, lit two new fires and tossed in the right leaves. He rolled two new cigars and lit one, his hands shaking all the while, then placed his box over one of the fires and sat with the livé cigar held close to his nose.

Soon he felt the smoke being drawn into his bottom and then expelled in a loud explosion. Immediately his arse stopped breathing and air began moving through his nostrils. He drew in a long, long breath, savouring it with great relief before looking across at Oilei, who was still giggling soundlessly and obviously in a state of shock. O God, he's off his rocker, Seru muttered as he moved over and led him with his box to the second new fire.

Seru lit the other cigar and held it under Oilei's nose. In a little while, when Oilei had begun regaining his senses and breathing normally, Seru returned to his own box.

Now that they had done the right thing, its effect began to overwhelm them. They sat zombie-like, completely lost in their respective worlds of heightened sensuality. Oilei closed his eyes, and as the smoke circulated down below, wafting through nooks and crannies and curling up rolling hills and into other things unmentionable, he felt and all but saw Makarita's honeyed hands moving oh so lightly through dales and vales and up the weeping willow tree on their nuptial evening. The smoke that he sniffed caressed his nostrils and floated langourously through the chambers of his sinuses then glided up the sides of his brain, giving him the sensation of Makarita's thighs rubbing delicately against his ears and the sides of his head while he was doing something unmentionable on the night of their honeymoon. There were many other things that Oilei and Seru felt, tasted, saw and smelled, and they all added up to the most extraordinary experience either man had ever had. Throughout all this, Oilei was oblivious of the revolutionary struggles that raged inside him.

When they returned to normality, the fires and the cigars were stone cold, the outside world was pitch dark and silent except for the chirping of crickets, and a lamp was glowing in the shed. Someone had obviously sneaked in and left it there. Oilei checked his watch, which said four o'clock. They had been away for over sixteen hours. They looked at each other and smiled weakly as they put on their clothes.

'This has been the most beautiful thing I've ever experienced.

If all revolutions were like this, I'd fight the bloody tuktuks anytime anywhere,' Oilei said contentedly.

'You can only do it five more times and that's it. We must suppress our desires and do what's necessary for the peoples of the world.' Seru laid a hand on Oilei's shoulder. 'Not a word to anyone about the accident, promise?'

'You can bet your arse on it,' Oilei replied.

They left the shed for the house, Oilei to his bedroom where he dozed off almost immediately; Seru to the spare bedroom where his people were sleeping on the floor. The old man returned to the lounge and sat there thinking about the marvel of the discovery. He was still at it when the birds broke out into songs as they ushered in the new dawn. A new dawn in the history of humankind, Seru told himself as he rose, stretched his arms and went into the toilet.

While he was washing his hands in the bathroom, Seru looked into the mirror and froze. His nose was brilliantly pink, setting itself off against the dark background of the rest of his face. He peered carefully again but there was no mistaking it. It was pink. He unhinged the mirror, laid it on the floor, switched on the light for greater illumination and squatted. His entire end region was shimmering grey, no doubt whatever about it either. O Christ, he muttered, his nose and presumably his brain had turned arse-coloured and his nether end brainwashed. The accident had done it; that stupid Oilei!

He was just about to bellow at his host when he remembered Oilei's final words during the ceremony. 'If anything goes amiss this time . . .' Seru knew that it was Oilei's fault, but he also realised that the ultimate responsibility was his. It was his medicine, and he had ruthlessly used a ceremonial situation to manoeuvre a most reluctant Oilei into his trap. Oilei knew it too; hence the veiled but unmistakable threat. He must put as much distance as possible between himself and the former boxing champion. He tied a handkerchief around his face, below eye level. Then he went into the spare bedroom and extracted from his wife's basket a pair of dark sunglasses, which he put on. Noiselessly he woke up every member of his family, signalling them to keep quiet. When they were ready they stole out of the

95

house and hastened away. They were about ten kilometres from the village when the first bus to Kuruti drove by.

At the capital Seru sent his family on to Rovoni, telling them that he would follow later. He went to the Jubilee Park and slept under a low bush that hid him from any casual glance. When it was dark he hurried to the waterfront and found a fishing boat with a fifty-horsepower Yamaha engine. Anglers or divers must have just provisioned it for a fishing expedition; there was sufficient food and water to last a whole week or more. Perhaps the owners had gone to fetch more provisions? Too bad; he took the boat.

Thirty hours later he saw an island and headed straight to the beach, where to his utter amazement he found Losana Tonoka, Marama Kakase, Domoni Thimailomalangi, many other *dottores* from Tipota, and hundreds of people he had not seen before, all stark naked, practising yoga and doing other things that boggled his mind.

Marama appeared to have shed at least thirty kilograms. She was trim and looking extremely fit for her age. Seru was so warmly welcomed that he decided to stay on.

He had landed on Nanggaralevu.

Oilei woke up after noon. He lay in bed basking in the afterglow of his remarkable treatment. Then all of a sudden his senses sharpened and he wanted Makarita urgently. He could feel her thighs moving against his ears and her hands active in his groin. He raised himself to call her and in the process saw his reflection in the mirror on the dresser a few feet from the foot of the bed. He could not believe what he saw. He shook his head and blinked his eyes, but there it was, a brilliant pink nose attached to his light brown face. He scampered on all fours to the foot of the bed for a close-up view, which only confirmed what he had seen. He pinched his nose and pulled it, hoping that it was false, but it would not come off. Then he remembered the accident and the breathing through the wrong orifice. He stood up, dropped his pyjamas and bared his buttocks at the mirror, only to find that his whole bottom was glistening grey.

Oilei was shocked and outraged. Seru had done it twice to him.

He jumped out of bed and shouted, 'I'll kill you, you fucking tuktuk!!!' as he ran into the spare bedroom.

'Where's that son of a bitch!! Rita!! Rita!!'

Makarita bolted out of her bedroom, where she had been mending a blouse, and streaked for the front door. Before she was halfway across Oilei grabbed her and spun her around. The look of utter terror in her face struck him and overcame his rage. He drew her gently to his chest, where she broke down and sobbed and laughed at the same time. She tried to pull herself away to look at him but he held her tight, averting his face.

'You brute! You beast! I thought you were going to kill me!!!'

She reached up and tore at his hair and scratched raw the back of his neck, and before they knew it they were in bed coupling away like a pair of teenagers.

Afterwards Oilei remembered. 'Where are they?' he asked, more from curiosity than anger.

'Who?'

'The Rovoni pigs.'

'Oh. They left before anyone else woke up. Must've been in a hurry to get away.'

'Just as well. I'd have done him in otherwise. Lucky bastard.' In a little while he added quietly, 'It was really my fault though,' and told Makarita everything that had happened. By then his wife was no longer shocked by the discoloration of his nose.

'So. The brain's seeped down and the arse's risen. You should be in a nut house,' she said, giggling wantonly.

'It was quite a revolution though. The top dogs are in exile among giant crab lice and the underdogs have taken over. Seriously, what can we do? I can't go around with this nose.'

'Bulbul,' Makarita suggested. 'We can always ask him. I'll go to the Health Centre and ring him up. But you'll have to earn it first.'

7

It was late in the afternoon when Bulbul arrived. He emerged from the driver's seat, walked to the other side and opened the passenger door. A tall, elderly, lean, white-haired and white-bearded man wearing dhoti and carrying a battered briefcase stepped out, took a deep breath and, escorted by Bulbul, walked lightly up the path toward the house.

Oilei watched all this from the open doorway, surprised at seeing his friend acting the chauffeur. But Bulbul, never known to kowtow to the wealthy and the powerful, always deferred reverentially toward holy men of all religions.

'I have brought the great yogi and sage, Babu Vivekanand, who most generously and graciously offers you his services. Babu, this is my best friend, Oilei Bomboki, of whom I have already told you,' Bulbul introduced them stiffly.

'The Creator of all things showers his blessings upon you,' Babu said. 'I have heard much about you and must say that I have been very impressed. I and my organisation owe you a great deal. Without knowing it, you have rendered us a great service. No. Do not ask any questions; things will be revealed in due course. It is an immense pleasure for me to have this opportunity to be of some use to you. Shall we go inside? Thank you.

'A good house you have here,' Babu complimented as he walked in. 'Very well ventilated. Ventilation is a necessary feature of any house. There should always be plenty of moving air in confined spaces. Aaah, chairs . . . No thank you. I prefer the floor. The surfaces on which one stands, sits or lies must always be firm and solid. Helps to keep the spine straight, thus encouraging good breathing and circulation.'

Babu lowered himself on the floor and effortlessly assumed

a lotus sitting posture. Oilei and Bulbul followed suit but sat cross-legged facing him. The sage kept his counsel for a while before he began with the authority of a physician in his surgery.

'Please remove the handkerchief from your face. Thank you. I can see what our friend meant when he gave an account of your problem. All problems in the world are connected, however disparate they may appear on the surface. There are no unrelated or unique problems. We isolate them from each other only because it is easier to deal with them separately. Therein lies an even bigger connected problem. Inasmuch as we deal with reality in piecemeal ways, in the long run we never find lasting solutions. What we always produce are short-term solutions that generate even bigger and more intractable problems.

'Take your illness, for example. Because you thought that only your anus was in trouble, you tried to find a cure for it. Yesterday, as our friend here informed me, you discovered that it was connected with problems elsewhere in the body, although the Rovoni expert misunderstood the real nature of the causes. There are no tuktuks. But your limited and distorted understanding of the larger ramifications of your anal problem is nevertheless evidence of the relatedness of things. We talk of things as if they are separate and unique. There is only a single reality, of which we and everything else are manifestations. We are united in the One Infinite, the Absolute Ground of Being. There are no separate existences. Keep this in mind while we deal with your particular case.

'The problem with your anus is rooted in the inherent human tendency to isolate and then divide manifestations of the One Infinite, in this instance, the human body, into different parts and assign to each of them different values. You and most of the rest of humanity look at parts of the body and say that some are good and beautiful and others bad and repulsive. You're proud of some and ashamed of others. You would not, for example, discuss the anus on the same level as the eyes. The body itself is a unity and together with the mind and the soul forms a larger unity of the being. You can go on from there indefinitely. The whole phenomenon is very complex and requires a great deal of intellectual effort to fully comprehend. We shall not go into it here, for most of it cannot be articulated through words. You will realise it more and more as you progress with yoga.

'All parts of the human body are of equal value. But you have, in your limited perception of reality, viewed them very differently. People have composed countless songs about the beauty of the eyes, the lips, the hands and the breast. But there is no music, no poetry that extols the merits of the anus. You can flaunt your face and other parts of your body, but if you dare bare your anus in public you will be apprehended for obscenity.

'You should already have noticed that I use the word "anus" and not "arse", which is loaded with the most repulsive connotations associated with a part of the body that is as good, as beautiful, as worthy of lyrical poetry as any. The anus is the most maligned, most unjustly loathed and abused part of the body. When people behave atrociously they are called arseholes. It is extremely reprehensible to compare the innocent anus with the dregs of society. Thoroughly obnoxious people are often called stinking arseholes. Yet they could easily be called stinking armpits or smelly mouths. These parts of the body surely discharge odours as pungent as those that come from any other parts. Also, filthy people are called dirty arseholes. The anus is as clean as any part of the body. And if you think objectively, you will see that the anus is always washed more thoroughly than any part of the body. Most people wash it too vigorously when showering, as if they were punishing it for being there or trying to rub it off. But the anus has the right to be where it is, and to be treated with respect and love. We treat our heads with respect and we call our leaders heads. We could, with equal felicity, call them anuses.

'The anus is like the lower orders of society. It does the most unpleasant jobs and no one would like their daughters to marry garbage collectors. It is class prejudice of the worst order. The great teacher, Jesus of Nazareth, once told his disciples to behave toward the least members of society as they behaved toward him. We must behave likewise toward our anuses. It is therefore necessary to review your whole attitude toward the anus. You must change and be convinced in your being that the anus is good, beautiful, lovable and respectable.

'You may recall that not many years ago Prime Minister Morarji Desai admitted to drinking his own piddle. Half the world was horrified and repulsed; the other half laughed. Almost everyone missed the great symbolic significance of the Prime Minister's behaviour; and that is, no part or product of the human being and therefore no human being is inherently repulsive and detestable. We must therefore bestow on the anus the dignity it has long been denied and restore it to its rightful and equal place among the honoured parts of our bodies. Only when you love and respect the rights of the lowliest member of your own body can you really love and respect the rights of the least members of your society. Mahatma Gandhi launched India on a new road by calling the untouchables "children of God" and giving them equal rights. We must do more by adding to the revered triumvirate of the body, mind and soul, the hitherto lowly anus.

'It is only when you are able to lovingly and respectfully kiss your own anus, and those of your fellow human beings, that you will know you have purified yourself of all obscenities and prejudices, and have overcome your worst fears and phobias. You will then be able to see with utmost clarity the true nature of beauty, which is the essence of the unity and equality of all things. For while you assign different values to different parts of your body and consider some of them dirty, disgusting and shameful, you will continue to assign the same values but with even greater intensity to similar parts of other people's bodies. That is, of course, a short route to hating and loathing them. Only when you treat every part of your body equally can you begin your journey toward true love. And once there, your life will harmonise with the One Infinite, and all your pains and agues will disappear. Sickness, disease and death strike us because of disharmonies in our existence. But when we synchronise our lives with the Eternal Programme of the Universe, we will live forever.

'You can now see what I mean by the interconnectedness of

all life and what happens when these connections are weakened or broken. I could continue along this line but it suffices for the moment that you have seen the broader context of your problem. There are practical steps you must take to reconcile your anus with the rest of your being and with the One Infinite so that you may be cured of your illness. These steps consist of two sets of yoga exercises.

'The first is relatively easy to master. The object is to enable you to see your anus closely for so often and for such prolonged periods that it is not strange and disgusting anymore. It will be as normal and familiar to you as are the palms of your hands; and to your nose, it will be as the fresh bud of spring. You will also marvel at the beauty of its structure and formation and at the rhythm of its movements. At the end of all this, you will have written a poem, "Ode To My Lovely Anus", which you may put to music and perform to rapturous audiences.'

Babu then paused and rose to demonstrate what he wanted Oilei to achieve at the end of the first series of yoga exercises. He took off his dhoti, folded it neatly and placed it aside, bent down very easily from the waist, hands behind him, placed his head between the unbent knees, parted his buttocks, and looked up at his anus. Oilei was enraptured by the old man's suppleness.

The yogi returned to his sitting position after he had put on his clothes.

'The second series of exercises will enable your nose to reach your anus,' he said as he stretched on his back and raised his legs and waist so that they were perpendicular to the rest of his body. Then he lifted his torso so that only the base of his spine remained on the floor. Following this, he spread his legs wide apart and bent his head until his nose touched his buttocks. Then slowly and gracefully he disengaged his head, lowered his body and returned to the sitting position.

'This second series of exercises will enable you to do what I have just done. They are not easy but if you do them conscientiously and properly you should be able to reach your goal in six to twelve months. You must remember that at your age your bones and muscles are stiff. But everything is possible given concentration and the will to succeed. You obviously had these qualities in your younger days; let us hope for the sake of your anus that you still have them today.

'When you get to the stage of being able to reach your anus with your nose, you will kiss it several times and, maintaining that position, meditate on it. You will then easily dispose of your revulsion and free yourself from the attitudes that inhibit your perception of the love that dwells in the unity of all things, and you will attain the state of harmony that will, by its very existence, cure you of all maladies. From that point on you will progress to higher things such as kissing other people's anuses. But you must obtain their consent first, and do it in complete privacy or you will be in trouble with the law. When this practice becomes widespread we will be in a position to press for law reform; and we will get reform just as other previously abhorrent practices have been legalised.'

Oilei could not understand all this; the very idea of bussing his own and other people's arseholes was most absurd and disgusting.

'Babu,' he said hesitantly, 'you said what you have said, but will you really act on it, like kissing your own arse, er, anus?'

'Of course. I've done it many times. Watch me carefully.'

And the great sage disrobed, stretched out on his back, raised the lower and upper parts of his body as before, spread his legs wide apart, used both hands to part his buttocks and buried his nose into it. He repeated the action several times in the most dignified and graceful manner before he put his dhoti back on and resumed his lotus position.

Utterly fascinated by the performance, Oilei said in all sincerity, 'Babu, will you kiss my anus?'

'Certainly, and most willingly. I had expected that request, as a matter of fact.'

Oilei disrobed and bared his bottom at the holy man, not quite certain that he would do it. But Babu rose into a kneeling position, parted Oilei's buttocks delicately, and in a reverential and sacramental manner, placed his nose inside. He drew back and repeated the action three more times before he resumed his lotus posture, saying, 'I have kissed your blessed anus with love and respect. If the presidents of the United States and the

103

Soviet Union do likewise at their next summit meeting, there will be no more threat of nuclear annihilation and there will be set an example for all the leaders of the world to emulate. As in most things we must begin from top down. When the top meets the bottom there will be eternal peace.'

Oilei noticed a change in the old man's demeanour as Babu paused before launching himself into something that seemed to have troubled him profoundly.

'The anus, as you have now seen, is neither revolting nor obscene. The most revoltingly obscene thing that we live with today is the threat of nuclear annihilation. It is obscene because of the spectre of destruction that it presents to all of us, but more so because it perpetuates, for as long as nuclear weapons exist, the fears, suspicions and hatreds that blind us to the beauty of creation; that is, the love, trust and respect that we can have for one another.

'Those who possess and control the most dangerous means of destruction have condemned themselves to live with increasing paranoia that breeds psychopathic behaviour; this may very well lead to their own undoing and the undoing of us all. They have spread that paranoia to their neighbours, satellites and client states. Every country that deals intimately with them has caught their incurable disease. The balance of terror they hold out to be the mainstay of peace means increasingly terrified populations, which know peace only as a precarious state of no war. Balance of terror is the most obscene invention of the human mind. Those who believe in it live in terror disguised as vigilance and will never find the serenity of mind and the true love of all life that are preconditional for a lasting peace. Those who control the most destructive weapons, those who allow their territories to harbour such weapons, and those who are directly and intensively influenced by them, are progressively psycho-pathically violent in every sense of the word. More and more they admire and worship violence and vengeful Ramboism.

'You are slightly fortunate in the South Pacific in that your relationships with them are not yet quite as intimate as others.' You must therefore keep them at arm's length so that you at least may maintain a semblance of civility and humanity that will make your conditions bearable. The purveyors of the balance of terror are sending their emissaries, their nuclear ships and submarines to your shores to draw you into the vortex of their paranoia, for they can neither conceive of nor tolerate the idea that there are human beings who are genuinely free and wish to remain free of the self-inflicted fears that are undermining the foundations of their societies. You must remember that the dinosaurs did not kill each other off; each was its own murderer.

'Only one country in your region has been sane and courageous enough to tell the purveyors of terror to keep their madness to themselves. You must join this country and try and join with men and women in the fear-racked, violent societies who are struggling to bring back some measure of sanity to our collective existence.

'One way of contributing to world peace, and this is where your seemingly unrelated and unique personal problem is in fact connected to global issues of great moment, is to spread the gospel that every part of the human body is beautiful and sacred in the eyes of the gods. We must begin from ourselves, from the lowest organs of our bodies, before we expand elsewhere. We must be able to celebrate the anus as we celebrate the mind and the heart and from there to proclaim that in the realm of the One Infinite we do not call people arseholes, buggers, cunts, dildos, fuckwits, poofters, shits, turds or wankers. We must greet, love and dance with each other in the middle of our zones of taboo, for we have not created any real taboos, only the fears and phobias that we, in our limitless capacity for self-delusion, have swept to the boundaries of our cherished conventions, where they remain to haunt us into insanity and violence.

'For you, Oilei, learn to love your anus and those of your neighbours and never again call them arseholes. Kiss your anus and theirs, and you are on the road toward contributing to the healing of our collective self.'

The great sage paused and extracted a manila folder from his briefcase and handed it to Oilei.

'In that are copies of exercises that you will do every morning. It will be months before you reach your goal, but always

105

keep in mind that long-term solutions are the best.

'Finally, you will from now on stop swearing and blaspheming. That will help to clear the fog in your mind and the stains on your soul. Some time after I leave, you will see a miracle.'

That evening Oilei was in bed, lost in his recollection of all that Babu had said and done, when Makarita tiptoed in, touched his groin and whispered loudly, 'Hey champ, let's do it . . . Shhh, cocky, did you hear me?' and tugged at the jackhammer.

'What?'

'I said let's fuck.'

'My dear Rita,' Oilei spoke from a great distance, 'we no longer use that word. It fogs the mind and stains the soul. You should have said, "Let us persuade our respective members to engage in a sacrament of love". That's the cleanest way of putting it.'

'Engage . . . our . . . members . . . in a sacra . . . oh shit! That's a load of crap!'

'We do not use those words either. Faeces are good, wholesome by-products that are essential to agriculture.'

'Agriculture? What's that got to do with turd?'

'Rita, my darling . . .'

'Don't my-darling me, you crazy arsehole!'

'Those aren't terms of endearment . . .'

'Endearment! What's wrong with you? Have you lost your fucking balls?'

'My sweet spouse . . .'

'Sweet spouse, for Chrissake! Talk sense! Do you or don't you want a screw?'

'Rita, Rita my beloved. Your name rings of the sounds of Eden. By all means, flap your wings, spread your limbs and shortly we shall be in Paradise engaging our respective members . . .'

'O Lord. You've really gone cuckoo this time. Forget that I asked you. Forget it! You're so romantic! I'm off sex for good! Do you hear me? I may as well join a convent!' Rita rushed out weeping with frustration.

Oilei remained still, contemplating the ceiling. He had been

106

a changed man since Babu the yogi anointed his anus. He lowered his eyes slowly and saw his reflection in the mirror. To his great delight his nose was no longer pink. He checked his bottom; it too had changed colour back to normal. It must have been a result of that kiss of love and respect, he told himself as he drifted off to sleep.

In the early hours of the morning, Makarita woke up to answer a call of nature. She entered the bedroom because she was surprised that the light was still on so late; Oilei was never a night owl. What she saw then convinced her that her husband had really gone around the bend. He was lying there fast asleep while his mouth was frozen in an act of kissing something. Most probably something disgusting, Makarita told herself.

A few hours later she stepped into the lounge to observe Oilei doing some strange exercises she had never seen before. In fact, since she had known him she had not seen him doing any physical exercises. Perhaps he did not need to, because hard work on the farm had kept him superbly trim. She guessed that he was exercising because of the long period of inactivity since his illness began.

'What're you on to now?' she asked.

'I'm doing yoga, my love.'

'Yoga?' Makarita had never heard that word before. Neither had Oilei until he met Babu.

'It's a special kind of exercise that enables people to do great things.'

'You're not taking up boxing again, are you?'

'Goodness gracious me, no, my beloved. It's something far more significant. Boxing is nothing by comparison. It's something that will contribute tremendously to peaceful intercourse . . .'

'You wouldn't have one with me last night . . .'

'I tried to approach it cleanly but you wouldn't listen. Anyway, what I mean is that what I'm doing will lead to something that will promote the advancement of peace in the world.'

'I don't understand.'

'The first series of yoga exercises will enable me to look at my anus.'

107

'Your what?' Makarita couldn't believe what she was hearing, especially her husband's avoidance of crude words.

'My anus, you know. It's a clean word that . . .'

'I prefer arse. But why would anyone want to look up his arsehole?'

'So that I may love and respect it.'

'Love and respect your own . . . no. You're pulling my leg.'

'Far from it, my sweet spouse, I . . .'

'Don't call me that again, you idiot. Makes me feel like I'm some spilled lemonade. Yuk!'

'Far from it, my dear. You see, when I love and respect my anus, I will kiss it.'

'Kiss your own arse? Sweet Mother of God!!'

'Most certainly yes,' Oilei asserted with the conviction of the born-again street corner preacher. 'And afterwards, I will love and respect your anus and kiss it too.'

'Kiss my arse you will, will you? Never!!'

'But that's not the end of the matter, you see. The time will come when you will love and respect my anus and kiss it too, because . . .'

'Me kissing your bleeding arsehole? I will do no such disgusting thing!! Never!! Urrgh. You make me sick!!'

'Oh, you will. You will, my beloved, when you see the beauty of . . .'

'Your filthy thing down there beautiful? You're out of your fucking nut!!

Makarita shrieked with laughter of the kind that comes only from those on the verge of a nervous breakdown. Realising what was happening, she checked herself. She must keep her sanity; Oilei was already over the edge.

'You kiss mine, I kiss yours. That's what you're aiming for, aren't you? What will the neighbours think?'

'Never mind the neighbours, my beloved. I will kiss their anuses too, and they will kiss mine . . .'

'And mine into the bargain, I suppose. So we're going to have a mass orgy, are we?'

'It will not be an orgy. It'll be the new eucharist. And if the presidents of the United States and the Soviet Union . . .'

Oilei stopped abruptly when Makarita, for no conceivable reason, began to shriek again and then crashed on the floor and lay still. He lifted her onto the divan, tucked a cushion under her head, checked her breathing, pulse and eyes, and slapped her lightly on the face several times. She opened her eyes, registered what she saw and passed out a second time. Oilei slapped her some more until she came to. This time utter horror and disgust stared into his face. She instinctively tightened her legs together, tucked one hand under her bottom and pushed Oilei away with the other.

'Go away. Don't touch me. Don't come near me.' She rose and edged away from him, still protecting her behind. She opened the front door and disappeared.

Oilei shrugged his shoulders and resumed his exercise.

8

'Go on please,' urged Dr Sigmund Benjamin Zimmerman, acting director of the St Martins Mental Hospital at Kuruti, the biggest of the eight such institutions in the country. Dr Zimmerman was an Austrian ('I'm not an Australian,' he always corrected people) on his first two-year contract at St Martins, sponsored by the World Health Council. He had been in the post for only three months after spending thirty years in just about every region of the Third World; this was his first posting to the South Pacific.

'But when he said that he was going to kiss the er, anuses of the presidents of the United States and the Soviet Union it was too much for me and I passed out until he had slapped me back into consciousness,' Makarita concluded her account lying on the couch.

After her escape from Oilei she had gone to the Health Centre and rung St Martins; Dr Zimmerman had told her to come at once.

'Tell me, doctor, am I out of my mind?'

'On the contrary. You're the first really sane person I've seen in this country,' Dr Zimmerman replied as he consulted his notes. 'By the way, did he once use the word "arse"?'

'No, doctor. He even corrected me for saying it.'

'That's a good sign. It means that he's not too perverted yet. His case may be an extreme form of anal fixation. Is he obsessively methodical and tidy?'

'Ha! On the contrary, doctor. You should see the mess he always makes. But it may be that he's developing, what do you call it? Anal something? He's cleaned up his language, you know. He was always swearing and blaspheming at the drop of a hat. It was his normal way. And last night when he spoke as if he

110

were the archbishop I knew straight away that he was going
cuckoo. But what's that got to do with anal fixing? Oh, yes.
Remember me saying he was trying to fix his eyes on his arse,
sorry, anus? Maybe that's anal . . .'

'Maybe,' Dr Zimmerman cut in, bringing to a full stop any
further unprofessional speculation. 'We must get him here. He
needs urgent medical attention. The problem must be nipped
in the bud before he starts going around making an ass of himself
or something worse.'

'I agree, but you see, doctor, he will never consent to be
admitted to a hospital. He's got this thing about nurses looking
up his arse.'

'He has, has he?' Dr Zimmerman's eyes lit up. 'Most interesting. His mother must have tickled him down there once too
often when he was a toddler. Most interesting indeed. That's
why it's imperative that we get him here as soon as possible.
He needs re-tickling down there to get rid of his unhealthy obsession. It will most certainly rid him of any other problems rooted
in the same infantile experiences. But how to get him here is
the big question. Let me think for a while.'

Dr Zimmerman went into another room and returned shortly
with a small tablet wrapped in tissue paper, which he gave to
Makarita saying, 'Put this in his drink. Any drink. It's completely odourless and tasteless and very easily dissolved. He'll
be knocked out for three hours. Ring me as soon as he's out.
If you can do it, say, early tomorrow morning, that'll be most
convenient all round. He must never suspect afterwards that
he was drugged.'

Early the following morning, after he had completed his exercises, Oilei asked his wife for a glass of water. He woke up in
a strange place lying on a couch. A small, bald-headed, elderly
man with a goatee and a nose like Losana Tonoka's was sitting
on a comfortable chair nearby, watching him.

'Where am I? Who are you?' he demanded, looking wildly
around.

'You're in hospital, Mr Bomboki. Don't worry, there're no
nurses around this part of the hospital. You will not be bothered

111

by any of them, I assure you. I'm Sigmund Zimmerman, your doctor while you're here. You were brought in an ambulance after you collapsed at home and wouldn't come out of it. You must have been exercising a bit too vigorously. We have checked you thoroughly and there seems to be nothing wrong apart from the draining abscess on your buttocks. I will not deal with it because it requires surgery, and that's a different department altogether. I hope that you will do something about it soon.'

'Thank you for your concern. I'm already doing something about it, as a matter of fact. It'll take time, but it'll heal very nicely without surgery. How did you know about my former attitude to nurses?'

'Former attitude, Mr Bomboki?'

'Yes. As a matter of fact I'm not at all concerned if they look me up. At the moment I'm preparing myself to look at it. Anyone else may look me up with love and respect. But how did you know?'

'You talked a lot while you were unconscious,' Dr Zimmerman replied sincerely, 'and revealed a great deal of yourself. That's why I'm dealing with you. I would like to discuss with you some of your problems. It will be as long or as short as you want it to be. Do you mind?'

'Not at all, doctor. You will have my full co-operation.'

'Thank you. Now, one of the curious things you did while you were unconscious was to giggle a great deal as if someone was tickling you. Are you in any way ticklish?'

'Not that much nowadays. Adults don't play tickles, that's why. But Rita, my dear wife that is, would sometimes tickle me in bed. Very childish, one would say. Did she come too? Thank God for that. Where is she?'

'In the reception room,' Sigmund Zimmerman replied and pointed toward the door leading to it. 'As a child, were you ticklish?'

'I suppose so. Children always tickle each other.'

'Try to remember an incident as far back as you can.'

'Of what, doctor?'

'Of being tickled, say, in the groin or the buttocks.'

'Who would've done that?'

112

'Your mother, for instance.'

'Please doctor, leave her out of this discussion. You may not know it but in our country we do not talk about our mothers.'

'Why?'

'It's taboo.'

'I see. Now, can you remember any incidents?'

'I can't. My memory's not that good. Marama Kakase, our famous curer, has a photographic memory. You should try her when she returns from Fiji. She'd be able to tell you everything that happened even before she was born. Er, why's tickling so important?'

'Because it has been scientifically demonstrated that those who are tickled down there too often grow up obsessed with their anuses. Some love their bottoms, others hate them. In both instances, very strongly and passionately.'

'And you think that I'm one of them?'

'I have yet to arrive at that conclusion. That's why I'm asking you.'

'Dr Zimmerman, any anal obsession, as you would put it, developed only recently, beginning with my illness. But only two days ago Babu, the great yogi and holy man, made me see why we should love and respect our anuses.'

'Enough to kiss them, is that so, Mr Bomboki?'

'Who told you that?'

'I'm an experienced man. I could deduce it from what you said. You also mumbled something about it just before you came to. However, the question remains.'

'One must love and respect the anus to the extent that one would kiss it. That would revolutionise human relations the world over, you see.'

'It certainly will if sufficient numbers of people do it. I agree entirely.'

'So you agree with me and Babu. Have you experienced yoga, doctor?'

'Yes. As a matter of fact, I'm a devotee of it. Picked it up in India. I lived there for six years.'

'So you have observed, loved and respected your anus and those of others. I'm so thrilled to have met you, doctor. I hope

113

to be able to kiss yours in due course.'

'Er, there are different kinds of yoga, Mr Bomboki. The kind that I practise leads one to contemplate Eternity, not a part of the human anatomy.'

'That's exactly what my yoga's about. You call it Eternity, I call it the One Infinite of which we are manifestations. It's the same thing. Eternity begins in the anus. Babu, bless his soul, says so. It is only when you look up through the anus with correct attitudes that you see the limits of Eternity, for it begins there, goes full circle and ends right back there. In short, doctor, Eternity begins and ends in the anus.'

'Well, er, that's a most profound Philosphy of the Eternal Anus. It could only have been developed by those who have been tickled too often in the buttocks by their mothers when . . .'

'Hold it there please, Dr Zimmerman. I ask you again please not to mention my mother . . .'

'I was talking about mothers in general. Surely . . .'

'You clearly implied it for mine.'

'Perhaps I did. I'm sorry. But Mr Bomboki, in my profession we need, if we are to be effective, to bring to the surface, for analysis and therapy, the intricacies of early mother/child relationships.'

'Please, Dr Zimmerman . . .'

'Your case, Mr Bomboki, is a rare one. It's a combination of anal fixation of an indeterminate form, and Oedipus complex.'

'What is Oedipus complex, doctor?' Oilei asked in the tone of voice of someone who had just woken up from a long, realistic dream only to find out that it was all an illusion.

'To put it simply,' Dr Zimmerman answered patiently to an F-grade student, 'the Oedipus complex is this. When you were a little boy, you hated your father and wanted to kill him so that you could have sex with your mother.'

Oilei rose slowly from the couch, towered over the seated Dr Zimmerman, grabbed him by the collar, lifted him clear off the ground with one hand and hissed into his face, 'You dirty little arsehole, if ever again I hear you utter the word "mother", I will personally kick your fucking arse all the way back to Vienna.' He dropped him none too gently on the floor, stalked

out into the reception room and dragged Makarita from her seat.
'Let's get away from this stinking shithouse.'

'What happened back there?'

'I nearly killed a bloody idiot.'

'What did he do?'

'Never mind. Let's go home and screw or something.'

'Welcome back to the world,' she said with relief.

'Fuck you!'

'Watch your language, shithead. What will Babu say?'

'Go kiss his arse!'

By the time they reached the bus station Oilei's mood had improved.

'How about dropping in on Bulbul?' he suggested.

Makarita knew better than to say no even if she wanted to, which on that occasion she did not. Whenever Oilei went to town he almost invariably dropped in on Bulbul, who was almost always home since that was also his business headquarters. He had converted half the front verandah of the old colonial bungalow into an office equipped with a desk, a chair, a telephone, an old filing cabinet he had rescued from the backyard of a renovated firm downtown, bookshelves strewn with spare parts and everything else except books, and a single bed pushed against the wall opposite the desk, which served as a bench for visitors and as a couch for Bulbul whenever he wanted to escape from his crowded household. There was also a wooden box by the couch on which stood a kava bowl that never seemed to be empty. Built in the 1920s on freehold land before Kuruti had grown from a port town into a bustling small city, the house stood on a larger than usual piece of residential land. The front lawn had become, by an unplanned process of transformation, a depot for taxis and trucks, while at the back was a growing junkyard with vehicles in various stages of being stripped for spare parts.

As soon as Oilei and Makarita appeared at the gate, Sumitra rushed up to them looking very agitated. At barely a metre and a half, she was fifteen centimetres shorter than her husband. She had greying hair and a frail appearance that belied the inner resilience she needed to cope with an unpredictable Bulbul and a brood of three sons and two daughters. All the children had married and had brought their spouses to live in the big house. Sons and sons-in-law were all drivers-cum-mechanics in the family business. Bulbul was the manager and head of a growing clan of more than thirty souls. He had long ago stopped counting the number of people in the house, only money for their thousand needs.

'There's something terribly wrong with him,' Sumitra said anxiously, pointing a thumb over her shoulder in the general direction behind her. 'He's been doing some strange exercises and saying shameful, disgusting things.'

'He's been talking about his arse, hasn't he?' Oilei asked.

'He now calls it anus. It sounds even more disgusting,' Sumitra spat.

'It's a neutral word and it's cleaner, much cleaner . . .'

'I don't care. I don't trust new words for the same dirty old things. He's gone crazy since yesterday. Please, you're the only one who can save him now. He won't listen to anyone else. The boys are very upset. I'm afraid that if he goes on the way he is, they might do something to him. I've been trying to calm them down, but they're hotheaded.'

'Silly bugger. Let's go in.'

They marched into the house and as Sumitra and Makarita went straight ahead, Oilei turned left at the verandah and opened the office door. Bulbul was sitting on the desk top trying very hard and unsuccessfully to lift his other foot for a complete lotus position.

'Well, well. Greetings brother! How's the exercise programme coming?' Bulbul broke out happily.

'You mean the arse development shit?'

'We no longer use unclean words, Brother Oilei,' Bulbul responded, changing his tone. 'They encourage the fog that blurs our vision of the One Infinite.'

'Look, you silly bugger. I was supposed to be doing that, not you. Remember?'

'The light of true knowledge illuminates everyone, not just the select few.'

116

'Oh, shit!'

'Sit down, please. Do not use words that stain our souls. Let's talk about our programme.'

'Look here, I had a programme, not you. Get that one straight. I don't have it any more. It's all crap.'

'But you let Babu kiss your anus . . .'

'Don't remind me of it again . . .'

'I saw your face when he did it. You looked so angelic that I decided there and then to enlist in the great cause. When I drove him home that afternoon, we went in and I . . .'

'You also let him kiss your arse?'

'With great love and respect he touched my anus with his nose. I felt so blessed. I really . . .'

'The man's a pervert, a bloody con artist!'

'Brother Oilei, you have reverted to your old ways . . .'

'And so should you. Get some sense back before someone else does it for you.'

'All the sense that I have is now in the service of humanity. This world of ours needs a new approach to peace. Babu has shown the way.'

'Babu's out of his fucking mind. He needs locking up. And so will you if you keep on going like that.'

'My dear brother, Babu's beyond it all. Sanity and insanity have no relevance for him. He's already so immersed in the Anus of the Universe that nothing will ever touch him. You can lock him up, but that will only cost the taxpayer unnecessary expenses.'

'I don't give a shit about Babu. It's you . . .'

'Please, Brother Oilei, refrain from using ungodly language. Babu has great trust in you and me . . .'

'He does, does he?'

'He has touched us both and has thereby anointed us his agents and recruiters in this country. I shall tell you a secret you must not under any circumstances reveal to anyone. Babu arrived here from overseas months ago looking for devotees for his yoga commune on Nanggaralevu, an island in Fiji. The commune operates behind a front called the International School of Traditional Medicine. Babu will explain everything to you. He has spent

117

a great deal of time in rich countries and has a lot of American and European money behind him. He said that Fiji's the ideal location for the commune and for the great work that he has been destined to do.

'Fiji's the hub of the South Pacific, and the Pacific will soon be the hub of the world. By starting in Fiji we will have the South Pacific, half the world's greatest ocean, at our disposal. There will be people from Tonga, Samoa, Niue, Cook Islands, Tahiti, Vanuatu, New Caledonia, Solomons, Kiribati, Tuvalu, Tokelau, Nauru as well as from Fiji, Australia, New Zealand and Papua New Guinea. We will also have the former Trust Territories of Micronesia, although they're in the North Pacific. All these countries are already well practised in the art of kissing anuses, although for a very different set of reasons from what Babu has in mind. Our commune will become a great new regional institution, strong and united unlike the tottering University of the Southern Paradise and the rest. Those institutions are disintegrating because of lack of any credible overall philosophy.

'By the way, yesterday Babu received a cable saying that old Seru Draunikau has just joined the commune. He's in good company. Losana and Marama are looking after him.'

'Good God! Those bogus *dottores* deserve to be conned. How on earth did that bloody tuktuk get there so soon?'

'We don't know the details yet, but he got there accidentally on a stolen fishing boat. Anyway, in our commune to which our fortunate compatriots have preceded us, we will build for the twenty-first century, during which the centre of world power and civilisation will shift forever from the Atlantic and the Mediterranean axis to the Pacific Basin. We will then expand our activities to cover the entire Basin from the Arctic to Antarctica, from the Americas to the Orient, providing it with a great unifying ideology for peace. We will conquer the centre of the world and from there convert the rest of humanity to our revolutionary philosophy of love and respect for the anus.

'Babu calls it the Pan Pacific Philosophy for Peace (PPPP), and our movement is called the Third Millenium. We, the members, are Millenarians. Think of the challenge, the thrill and the magnitude of the task! The Pan Pacific Philosophy for

Peace and the Third Millenium will shake the twenty-first century and beyond as Marxism and Communism have shaken the twentieth!

'This is our great objective. We have to start from a small beginning, like the tiny seed from which the mighty mango grows. We will have a few academics from the University of the Southern Paradise to help us initially. Babu says so. They are the best and most experienced theorists of anything Pan Pacific. They will make superb Millenarians. And keep this top secret; don't tell anyone or the CIA will get you. Right?'

'You mean the CIA's in on this?'

'CIA's in on everything and everyone. So's the KGB. They're competing for Babu's favours, for they've seen the great wave of the future. Both have been kissing Babu's anus – for the wrong reasons of course – and he doesn't like it one little bit. But he lets them do it because he wants them to become used to it. Before long they'll be working for our great cause as real Millenarians, not as the spooks that they are now.

'Anyway, Babu has detailed information on every academic at the University of the Southern Paradise. Came from a mole dug deep in the Vice-Chancellor's office. He'd been leaking information happily to the press for years and no one at that university's been smart enough to catch him. But the CIA ferreted him out and he's been working for us since.

'Babu says that the best prospective Millenarians are some professors and the head of a particular department. The chief sociologist, er, head of department that is, is by far the best. He's a great Buddha-like figure, except that he's too hairy and so uncouth. He needs a thorough scrubbing with sandsoap, especially in the mouth. That's no problem, however; we'll shave his whole face and head and clean up his image.

'He's a hopeless head of department. Lets everyone manipulate him or stand on him. His books were written by his white wife; so was his PhD thesis. He's a pathetic hen-pecked husband; a most incompetent head of his household. He's got no mind of his own. That's why Babu thinks that he's so good for our purposes. His mind's a blank sheet, which we'll fill with great ideas and he'll come out real good. We may even make

119

him our first Hero of the Third Millenium. He's been approached with appropriate inducements, not money or anything crude like that but something much, much better. And he's amenable, very and most amenable. He's got the most beautifully tattooed anus for the Third Millenium. We'll take a drawing of it and use it as our logo. It'll serve humanity for the whole twenty-first century and beyond. He's thrilled with the idea. Immortality! But don't tell anyone or the KGB'll get you.'

'Do you believe in all that horseshit?' Oilei asked incredulously.

'You have regressed very badly, Brother Oilei. Babu will fix all that because he sees in you a potentially great shining anus for the Third Millenium. Should be here any time now.'

'Is he coming here?'

'Indeed. Any time now. Expect a miracle when he arrives.'

'No thank you. Shit on his face for me, will you? I'll be back tomorrow. I won't lose you to a purveyor of horseshit after all these years.'

Oilei stomped out, grabbed Makarita, pecked Sumitra on the forehead and left.

'What was that all about?' Makarita asked indignantly.

'Babu's expected there any minute. I don't want to meet him or I'll break his fucking neck. Bulbul's in dire need of help, the silly bugger. I'll be there tomorrow. One way or another I'll get him back. Won't let anyone destroy him. Never!'

After he had simmered down, Oilei said softly, 'I've been lucky to get out of it in time. Hope it's not too late for him, poor bugger.'

'You care very much for him, don't you?'

Oilei merely gave her the kind of look that always seemed to infuriate and reassure her simultaneously.

'I hate you,' she added without much conviction.

Next morning Oilei was just about to leave for Kuruti when Bulbul staggered out of his car. He had minor cuts to his face and mouth and a black eye. Oilei helped him inside and took off his shredded shirt. Although his body was covered with welts from a severe beating, there were no broken bones, no apparent internal injuries.

'Who did this to you? I'll kill the bastards!'

'My sons. The three boys I brought up with my own sweat and saliva. They wouldn't see reason. I pleaded with them to join me and Babu.'

'You did what? No wonder. I told you someone's bound to beat some sense back into you. Tell me everything. Rita! Get some hot water and dressings, please. This idiot's been messed up by his own boys. Serves him bloody right, too!'

'I've left home for good,' Bulbul announced plaintively. 'Even Sumitra and the girls sided with them. I'm staying here until the day after tomorrow. Then I go to Fiji with Babu.'

'What on earth for?'

'To join the commune. I'll give your love to Losana and Marama.'

'Oh, shit. Look, you're staying here; you're going nowhere without my say-so. Do you hear me?'

'But I must. Babu needs me; and you too, for that matter. But it's so very sad that you've regressed. Babu isn't worried though. He said that once the kiss of life has been bestowed on anyone's anus, he will always return to the fold. You will, because he's kissed you. You'll never forget that act of love and respect. It may take time but you will come back to us. You've been branded ineradicably with the Mark of the Third Millenium.'

'You haven't changed one bit. Even after the beating. We'll take care of that later. Now tell me everything. Start from when I left you yesterday.'

Makarita joined them, attending to Bulbul's cuts while he filled them in on what had happened. Babu did not turn up till late in the afternoon, Bulbul said. He told Bulbul that he was leaving for Fiji and would like him and Oilei to accompany him. Bulbul said that he was willing to but that he'd better forget Oilei, who'd reverted to his old ways. It was then that Babu told Bulbul not to worry about Oilei for he would sooner or later return to the fold. At dinner that evening Bulbul tried again to tell his family about the wonders of Babu's philosophy, but they shouted him down and the boys would have attacked him then but for their mother. No one would hear him out. In the morning at breakfast he announced his trip to Fiji with Babu. The boys rose in unison and went out. They returned shortly; one was armed with a stick, another with a length of hose, and the third brandished a clenched fist. He had no chance. He looked to Sumitra for help but she was egging them on; so were the girls. He managed to escape, got into one of the taxis and drove to the police station.

'You went to the police? Oh, shit! You've opened a can of worms. What did they say?'

'The police? They just laughed and offered to take me to St Martins.'

'Why didn't they? The stupid pigs!'

'I told them to forget I'd ever been there. And here I am, half murdered by my own family, laughed at by the police, and addressed in unclean ways by my very own brother!'

'And you deserve everything dished out to you,' Oilei interjected. 'You didn't tell the police about me, did you?'

'I didn't get around to that. I was going to say something but they just laughed me out. I feel very sorry for them . . .'

'You should feel sorry for yourself more than you're doing now, you silly bugger. Are you really certain you didn't mention my name?'

'I wouldn't lie to you. It'd only stain my soul,' Bulbul said simply.

Oilei went outside to think. He must stop Bulbul from going to Fiji but could not think of an effective and safe way of doing it.

Late in the afternoon Oilei emerged from his bedroom to find Bulbul sitting in a half-lotus on the floor, trying to lift the other foot to complete the posture. He rested and tried again, then saw his friend standing there watching him.

'I'm trying to do the full lotus before we leave. I'm not good at sea; I get dizzy and woozy whenever I'm on a boat. Babu said that the lotus is very good for sailing. Keeps the body in perfect balance and thus prevents seasickness.'

'So you're sailing to Fiji sitting lotus fashion all the way, is that it?'

'No. We're flying and then catch a boat in Suva for the island. The sea's quite rough this time of the year, so the lotus will come in handy.'

122

It was then that Oilei saw clearly the way to stop Bulbul and to get him out of his madness. It was beautifully simple and brilliantly cruel. But he had to do it. He smiled happily as he moved in on his friend.

'Here, let me help with that foot,' he offered.

'Don't. I have to do it myself.'

'Let me help or I'll swear blue murder at you.'

'OK, Brother Oilei. But do it gently and slowly. Easy does it.'

Oilei bent down and took Bulbul's unengaged left foot near the toes and lifted it slowly. Then suddenly, as quick as lightning, he tightened his grip, yanked and twisted hard. Ankle and knee joints cracked, and even before Bulbul opened his mouth, Oilei grabbed the trapped right foot and yanked and twisted again. It was the work of a heavyweight champion mercilessly systematic in destroying his opponent. Everything happened within a few seconds, accompanied by Bulbul's scream of agony.

'Shit!! You fucking arsehole!! You've broken my legs!!' All the most luridly obscene words came tumbling out over one another.

Satisfied with his performance, Oilei sat on the divan as if on the stool in his ring corner, watching the writhing, screaming Bulbul dispassionately. It's just as well Rita's not here or I might have had to deal with her too, he told himself. After several minutes when Bulbul had screamed and sworn himself hoarse, Oilei rubbed it in.

'Such language is not spoken in this house. It stains the soul and fogs the atmosphere. You should be ashamed of yourself for regressing to your filthy old ways, Brother Bulbul.'

'I'll kill you, you son of a bitch!' Bulbul promised painfully.

Oilei rose to the sound of the bell ringing in the second round, stepped over Bulbul, grabbed his left ankle and pressed, not very hard this time but enough to set Bulbul off screaming and swearing almost without sound.

'Listen, are you still going to Fiji with that arsehole?'

'For Chrissake, no!'

'Promise?'

'Yes, you fucking bastard, let go of me for God's sake!'

'What's Babu Vivekanand?'

123

'He's an arsehole!! Please let go of me.'

'Repeat what you said!'

'He's a fucking arsehole!! Please, please . . .'

Oilei dropped the foot. Bulbul was convulsively sobbing his heart out. Oilei knelt and lifted his face. The fanatic's look had been replaced by the most piteous sight of a normal human being weeping in agony. He lowered the head gently, rose and turned his back. In a little while he carried Bulbul out into the car, laid him as comfortably as he could on the back seat, and drove to Kuruti. Not a word passed between them.

At the hospital he located Dr Tauvi Mate, who immediately took charge. Bulbul was anaesthetised, his joints reset, plastered and put in traction. When he woke up he moaned in agony for he had no pain-killer. Oilei went out to a public telephone, made a call and returned to the bedside. Twenty minutes later Mr Lee walked in.

'Ah so!' he exclaimed, 'Good old Bulbul had an accident! Most unfortunate, ha! No pain-killer in this great national hospital? Most ridiculous, ha! But don't worry my friend, Lee Ho Cheung will fix you good and proper. So! I put two needles on each wrist. First needle, so! Second needle, so! Please don't move that wrist. Now, the other one. First needle, so! Second needle, so! I twiddle them and the pain goes away, OK? Has the pain gone? Not yet? So! I twiddle some more. Uh ha, gone now? All of it? Good, very good, ha! I come back in two days and do more twiddling. OK? So! Have a good rest, there will be no more pain till then.

'Ah so! You, my friend, how's your problem down there? Not so good? Still draining? We'll fix it up yet. So! You were supposed to come this morning, was that not so? You forgot? No problem! People always forget this and that, ha! And the pain? Coming back slowly? We fix it right away. Oh, ho, ho! No, no! Not in the hole! We do it on the ankles just like the other day, remember? Good! Needles in the hole only for draining, ha! We do it only in my surgery. We do it here and nurse finds out, we go to the clink for poofting! Not so very nice, no?

'Please lie on the floor at once. We do it quick time before

124

nurse comes. Too much trouble trying to explain acupuncture to damn, shit-ignorant doctors without their own pain-killers, ha! Ready? Right. One needle on the left ankle, so! One needle on the right ankle, so! I twiddle them both at the same time, so! Not so easy squatting and working on the blurry floor, ha! Much better on the couch. Pain's gone? Sure? Good. Ah so! You pay me next time you come to my surgery. Four days from now. Don't forget this time!

'See this? It's a jar of ginseng. You take. No charge. Free gift from Lee Ho Cheung, the only ginseng merchant in the whole blurry country, ha! Try that one, if you like some more, you pay for the next. Any friend of Bulbul's, Ah So's best friend, ha! You put tiny wee spoon in your tea and drink it. In quick time it gives you great powers to eat up four fine fillies all at the same time, one on top of another, so to speak only, ha! Friend Bulbul's fast asleep. Good sign, so! And good night to you, ha!'

Soon afterwards, seeing that his friend was resting comfortably, Oilei left quietly, closing the door behind him. He drove to Bulbul's, where he found Sumitra and the adult members of her family sitting on the verandah as if after a funeral. When he had told them where Bulbul was and what had happened, the gloom that had hung over them lifted. Surendra, the eldest son, went to the office and came out with the kava bowl. They drank and talked happily, and even made jokes of the things said by their father. Much later Oilei, who had been rather quiet, said, 'You all go tomorrow and visit him. He'll be happy to see you, he's got his senses back.' With that piece of advice he rose and Surendra drove him home.

The following evening, long after the visiting hour, Bulbul was fast asleep when the door opened quietly and a white-haired, white-bearded figure in dhoti slipped in. He stood at the foot of the bed watching Bulbul with great affection and tenderness. Then he reached out, pulled at Bulbul's pyjama pants and, with profound love and respect buried his face between the suspended legs.

'Oh, shit! Go away, you disgusting bastard! Fuck off! Nurse!! Nurse!!' But his voice was still too hoarse to carry much beyond the bed. He reached down and pushed Babu's head to no avail,

125

swearing blue murder. At that very moment a night nurse who happened to be passing by peeked in. What she saw caused her legs to move like windmill blades in a storm. In a very short time heavy footfalls pounded down the corridor and three hefty security guards burst into the room, taking Babu completely by surprise. The rest was swift and effective. Babu found himself on his stomach on the floor, both hands locked behind his back, his mouth firmly taped. The police arrived, took him to the station and questioned him until they decided with much disgust that they were dealing with a raving lunatic. They drove him to St Martins Hospital and left him there.

A month after the hospital incident, Dr Zimmerman received a surly American and a grim-faced Eastern European who had gone to St Martins to claim the yogi. Before the three of them left, Dr Zimmerman bolted his office door, dropped his pants and presented his anus to Babu, who knelt reverently and blessed it with his nose. The CIA and KGB agents were so pleased that they too added their blessings upon Dr Zimmerman.

'I shall see you in Fiji as soon as my resignation is accepted,' Dr Zimmerman said as he let them out.

Oilei and Bulbul saw no more of Babu in Tipota. But neither could erase the memory of the kiss that Babu had given them, for the seeds that he had sown in their anuses had grown in their minds to remain there haunting their souls until at last they admitted the truth about the nature of the universe.

## ◆9◆

Sixteen weeks had come and gone since Babu left St Martins Mental Hospital and vanished into the larger world. Bulbul had come out of the General Hospital and back into the management of the family business and household. He walked with a slight limp and with the aid of a cane, confident that within a month he would be his old self once again.

He had just that day told Oilei of the bad news. Ah So would not in the foreseeable future treat him again because he was neither in Kuruti nor even in Tipota. He had gone to Australia to retrieve his erring wife, who had preceded him there without his say-so but with the utmost secrecy and indelicacy in the company of a person of the opposite sex who, like her, was of a much tenderer age than her husband. The said person, one Mr Lee Kwang Soo, was the prodigal son of a prosperous restaurateur of the famed Dixon Street, Sydney, who was a second cousin of Ah So. Lee Kwang Soo had spent his annual three-week vacation leave as an honoured guest of the Lee Ho Cheung household, located on the top floor of the three-storeyed House of the Dragon Balm. His host had told him on his arrival, 'All I have is yours. Feel free and help yourself, ha!'

Lee Kwang Soo did indeed help himself most generously, in particular to his hostess, behind his host's back and on his host's bed; on the day of his departure his hostess drove him to the airport, Ah So being fully occupied in his surgery. Ah So recalled, when it was already too late, that before they drove off his own wife, Mee Chow, had hugged him, saying tearfully, 'Look after yourself for me, choochoo, I'll be back.' Little did he know! That evening he found the car abandoned at the airport and the Qantas departure list for its only flight to Australia that day showed that one Mrs Lee was on the flight on a first-

127

class ticket and was allotted a seat next to her handsome husband, Mr Lee Kwang Soo. Ah So followed on the next flight
out. 'See this?' he told the friend who had driven him to the airport, brandishing a duty-free barbecue skewer. 'When I catch
that son of a bitch, I'll stick this up his arse and twiddle it slowly,
very slowly, ha!' A week later the same friend received a telex
that read, 'Naughty kids not yet caught stop will return when
mission accomplished regards Lee Ho Cheung.'

This was bad news indeed for Oilei. 'People like that should
be hanged by the balls!' he told Bulbul, clenching and twisting
his fist. The regular acupuncture treatment had effectively
stemmed the pains in the arse and the head, and had helped to
keep the home atmosphere relatively pleasant. Now that Ah So
had gone the pains had returned to torture him as before. He
tried to find relief from others, but by then no *dottore* would touch
him for fear of losing his or her reputation and therefore
clientele. There was already an oversupply of curers and healers,
which was leading to stiff competition.

Even at that stage, when, after his experience with Babu, Oilei
had shed his objections to nurses seeing his private parts, he
could not change his mind about going to hospital. Dr Tauvi
Mate had advised him against entering the 'doors of death'.
Tipotans with means sent their relatives abroad for treatment.
Oilei had no means; gifts to *dottores* had virtually exhausted his
resources.

He grew so desperate and so quick-tempered that Mere
stopped going to his house, while Makarita spent half of every
day at her mother's. Stories of their steamy rows spread widely,
reaching even the Prime Minister, who was already concerned
with the effect of Oilei's notorious arse on the party image. The
Prime Minister called a special meeting of the party executive
and announced his withdrawal of Oilei's nomination to the long-
vacant Senate seat, declaring, 'We don't need another big
arsehole in Parliament; we have too many already. All agreed?'
'Yes, sir!' the party officials chorused – the only words they
dared use in his presence.

The news was the final humiliation for Oilei. Any measure
of relief during this period he found only when he thought of

Babu and the seeds he had sown in his anus. He always struggled to erase such disgusting thoughts but the more he tried, the more he pondered on them. He often wished that Babu was still around. He was at the nadir of despair when Bulbul and Dr Tauvi Mate visited him late one morning.

'How are you?' Bulbul asked.

'What do you think? Oh shit!'

'You must have an operation,' Dr Mate suggested.

'At the General? You're joking.'

'Not here. In New Zealand.'

'Shit! I've got no fucking money to get me there, let alone pay the bloody bills!'

'That's no problem,' Bulbul intervened. 'The Kiwi aid programme provides for sending medical cases to New Zealand. I just heard about it last night at a cocktail party. Tauvi's confirmed it.'

'Then why the bloody hell didn't you tell me about it before?' Oilei demanded, turning on Tauvi Mate.

'It didn't occur to me then . . .'

'You forgot! No wonder people die like flies in your bloody hospitals!'

'It's not something we broadcast around . . .'

'Then who do you fuckwits inform? Only people like you?'

'Come off it, you bastard. Tauvi's here because I asked him to help out. So shut up and listen.' Bulbul was the only man who could tell Oilei off and get away with it. 'Tauvi will write a report on your condition and recommend treatment overseas. Someone get the secretary of the village council to write a letter to the New Zealand High Commission asking for their help. I'll take the documents to the High Commission this afternoon. We must move fast.'

'How long do I have to wait?' Oilei asked hopefully.

'Depends on the High Commission and on the availability of beds in hospitals down there,' Tauvi Mate replied. 'They're always full and have long waiting lists for surgery. But often they make special provisions for patients from the Islands. I think it'll be anything between two days and two weeks before you can leave.'

'What're my chances?'

'As good as any, I suppose,' Tauvi Mate answered noncommittally.

'You don't sound optimistic. Oh shit!'

'We do our best and wait. OK?'

They set to work immediately. Tauvi Mate examined Oilei and wrote his report in the form of a letter to the village council. Bulbul went looking for Constable Butako, the council secretary, to write his application.

The Secretary
Korodamu Village Council
Central West District

Dear Sir,

I have just examined your chairman, Mr Oilei Bomboki, and discovered that he has an acute case of fistulitis, which needs emergency surgery by an experienced specialist. As facilities for such a delicate operation are not adequately provided for in this country, I recommend that Mr Bomboki be sent to New Zealand for treatment. If you can find means to send him overseas, I will be happy to contact a doctor I know in Auckland who will handle the case.

Yours sincerely,

Dr T. Mate, Dip.Vet.Sc.
Senior Medical Officer, Kuruti General Hospital

The High Commissioner
New Zealand High Commission
Paradise Towers, Kuruti

Dear Excellency,

We thank Lord Jesus for guiding us through the temptations of Satan to this beautiful and wonderful day. We praise Him also for His loving kindness in bringing you, Excellency, to our beloved country to help us become rich so that one day we will shake your hands and say 'hello' in the eye as a proud and self-sufficient people.

130

As for now we are poor and our hospitals are no good. They're so bad that our dear Dr Tauvi Mate, who works in our biggest hospital, told us not to go there because they will only kill us if we do. Better go to New Zealand, he said. But we have no money to go and we hear that you have lots of it to send us to your hospitals. We want you to help only one of us.

I am sure that you, Excellency, like everyone else, have heard of the great chairman of our village council, our beloved Oilei Bomboki, who is in a very big trouble with his oomfoo, I don't know how to say it in English, sorry sir. Dr Mate will tell you all about it. You know, sir, that our beloved chairman is the second most famous man in our country. He's still our greatest ex-heavyweight champion and he knocked out your champion three times in a row, sorry sir. Boxing and rugby are the most important things in our traditional culture as our beloved Prime Minister says, and Oilei is our living national culture hero, next only to the Prime Minister. If he was still young he would also be our greatest champion in the new sports of Kung Fu, Karate and Tae Kwan Do, but he is getting old and has this problem in his oomfoo. We want to send him to New Zealand but our council has no money. It used to have lots of it until last year when our treasurer, Sanovabitsi, disappeared with every cent. He is now living in your country and I feel most sorry for New Zealand because he is a very, very worst man. You tell your police to catch him and send him back to Korodamu because we want to beat him up real good and then send him to gaol.

So we have no money and Oilei has even less. That Chinese crook, Ah So, who used to treat Oilei and also the Prime Minister, has lots of money and has gone to Sydney chasing after his young wife who took off with his nephew and and I don't blame her because he's a dirty old man.

That's why I'm writing this letter on the behalf of the Korodamu Village Council to ask you, Excellency, to please give some money to Oilei to go to Auckland for an operation. We feel most sorry for him because he's in big pain and he gets cross very quickly and two days ago he tried to kill me when I said jokingly that he was a pain in the oomfoo. I jumped out of the window and ran like hell, praying to Lord Jesus to turn my feet into a motorbike and I'm very lucky to be alive today. But we all love Oilei and don't want him to die yet and also don't want him to kill anyone yet, especially me. So please give him some money to go to New Zealand.

Bulbul told me never ever to tell you this, but if you pay Oilei's trip to Auckland and also his medical bills it will only be fair and square, because part of the money stolen by Sanovabitsi was used for buying tickets from your Air New Zealand and he's spending the rest of it in Auckland. I promised Bulbul never to tell you so I've told you only a little bit. Please don't tell him that I told you or he will try to kill me although I'm a police officer. People here have no respect for law and order or for me so maybe I will try to go and live in New Zealand and do something else. No more policing for me. I will write you another letter about it may be soon.

If you pray to Lord Jesus, sir, He will tell you that the best and kindest and onliest thing to do is to help our beloved Oilei's oomfoo to become well again.

God bless you, Excellency.

Yours faithfully,

Constable D. Butako
Secretary, Korodamu Village Council

Butako sealed the letter together with the other one and Bulbul took it to the High Commission late that afternoon. It was channelled to Robert Ainslie, the newly arrived immigration officer, who consulted his Pocket Oxford Dictionary but could not find 'fistulitis'. It was then that John Johnston, the first secretary, staggered back from a three-hour lunch with some businessmen trying to export traditional wooden swords to New Zealand.

'Hey, Jack. What's fistulitis?' Ainslie called out, offering him the letters.

Johnston had difficulty focusing his eyes on the documents. 'It's easy, Bob,' he said at long last. 'Someone's having problems with his fists. Must've punched too many heads in his day. Well, well! A culture hero, is he? If I were you I'd write and tell them to try the Aussies. They have funds for culture preservation. They may very well stuff him up for the museum. You

132

can never tell with Ockers. Anyway, fist problems aren't serious enough to warrant an assisted trip to Auckland, I'd say.'

'You're right, Jack. Thanks.'

'Stupid buggers. Fancy trying something like that on us!'

'Oh, by the way. What do you think of the council letter? How'd you deal with it?'

'We get them all the time. Especially from the countryside and outer islands. I'd reply in the usual way but add a few tactful things to keep them happy. You've got to adjust to local ways of doing and saying things. You'll get used to it.'

'I don't know. Thanks anyway.'

It was well past four and most people had gone home when Ainslie walked into the reception room where Bulbul had been waiting patiently by himself. Ainslie handed him a sealed envelope saying, 'Sorry for keeping you waiting. These things take time. I'm afraid we can't do anything about your friend. If it had been anything more serious than his fists, there wouldn't have been any problem getting him away.'

'I don't understand. What fists are you talking about?'

'Your friend's problem with his hands. Dr Mate's report says "fistulitis". Must've punched too many heads in his boxing days. Sometimes old injuries don't surface until aeons later. Should be able to get him treated by a local chiropractor or a traditional masseur if you still have them. The Maoris certainly do. We don't send minor cases to New Zealand.'

'I don't know anything about fistulitis. But Oilei's hands are perfectly all right. It's his bottom . . .'

'You mean he was punched in the bottom?'

'Nothing like that, sir. He's suffering badly from pain inside his bottom. That's the problem.'

'Aha! A pain in the arse. Why didn't the doctor say so? Our High Commissioner's in Auckland with the same problem. He went last week, has been operated on and he's recovering fast. Painful thing, fistulitis, if that's what it means. Come back tomorrow morning with a more detailed medical report and we'll get the ball rolling. There shouldn't be any problem if it's pain in the, er, anus. See you then.'

Oilei, Bulbul and Constable Butako sat in the lounge, listening to Dr Tauvi Mate reading out Ainslie's reply.

Constable D. Butako
Secretary, Korodam Village Council
Central West District

Dear Constable Butako,

Thank you for your letter to the High Commissioner. I am sincerely sorry to hear that your chairman is so unwell. I hope that he will recover soon. Our policy is to help the very serious cases that cannot be treated here. I therefore regret to inform you that Mr Bomboki's condition falls outside that category for I have been advised that his fists could very well be treated locally.

I understand your personal situation for which you have all my sympathy. Your letter is and will always be treated with strictest confidentiality. You may depend on it.

With best wishes.

Yours sincerely,

R. Ainslie
Second Secretary, Immigration

'So he thought fistulitis is a disease of the fists! How could a New Zealander not know his own language well? Bloody idiot! Oh shit!'

'You can't blame him. He's not a doctor. Every field in their society has its own special words,' Dr Tauvi Mate explained. 'As Bulbul said, he was very sympathetic when he knew what your real problem was. Specially in view of his boss's similar pain. It's late already and I'm very tired. Let's get things done as he suggested. I'll write another report, and Butako writes another letter to go with it.'

Mr R. Ainslie
Second Secretary, Immigration
New Zealand High Commission
Paradise Towers, Kuruti

134

Dear Mr Ainslie,

I have examined Mr Oilei Bomboki and confirmed that he has an acute case of anal fistulitis, a condition of infection in the anal canal leading to the development of perianal abscesses that discharge pus from the infection. This condition can cause considerable discomfort, popularly known as 'pain in the arse'. It can only be corrected by a very delicate operation, which must avoid damaging the vital rectal muscles that control bowel motions. As you may have already known, there is a case pending in the Supreme Court concerning error in an operation that led to the plaintiff's total loss of control of his bowel movements. Given the state of medical facilities in our hospitals, no successful anal surgery can be guaranteed.

Mr Bomboki has two continuously discharging sinuses on each anterior quadrant. He is in constant agony and feels worse every day. It is necessary that he receives treatment overseas. Your assistance in this matter will be of great humanitarian value.

Yours sincerely,

Dr Tauvi Mate, Dip.Vet.Sc.
Senior Medical Officer, Kuruti General Hospital

Mr R. Ainslie
Second Secretary, Immigration
New Zealand High Commission
Paradise Towers, Kuruti

Dear Sir,

We praise Lord Jesus for leading us again into this wonderful day and for His love for us awful sinners. May the Lord be praised also for guiding you to reply very kindly to my letter to the High Commissioner, who, I'm most sorry to hear, is in New Zealand recovering from an operation in his oomfoo. It seems that only great and important people suffer from this kind of problem and our beloved chairman, Oilei Bomboki is, as you know, a great and important person.

I don't blame you, sir, for not knowing what an oomfoo is, because I also don't know the English word for it! But it certainly doesn't mean fist, which, in our language, is tooky. Oomfoo means the bottom hole that everyone was born with. Often that hole makes poofpoof, which is when bad air comes out of it sometimes quietly, sometimes loudly, but never smells nicely. Oilei has trouble with his hole, very painful, like I said in my letter to your boss who's recovering from the trouble with his own great big hole. Dr Tauvi Mate says there are two more holes growing inside poor Oilei's bottom. He's most confused about all three of them and finds it nearly impossible to tell which is the one that God gave him when he was born. So please give our beloved chairman some money to go to New Zealand for an operation because if he goes on being confused he'll go mad one day and kill someone. If you read my first letter again you will find other reasons why he should go to Auckland.

Thank you very much, sir, for not telling Bulbul what I wrote in my first letter. You New Zealanders are so very good at keeping confidences to yourselves because you don't gossip. It's not so good here, in fact it's very bad. Our famous but not so beloved Marama Kakase says that the teachers at our university are the worst ones; their mouths leak like the roofs of their libraries and lecture theatres. Many New Zealanders among them have very leaky mouths too but this is because they have picked up our bad habits. We all know that you don't gossip in New Zealand and that's why I want to go and live forever in Auckland soon. I will write you another letter about that.

If you pray sincerely to Lord Jesus, He will tell you again that the best and kindest and onliest thing for you to do is to help our beloved Oilei go away for an operation so that his new holes will be sewn up and the real one God gave him when he was born will become well again and do its job properly.

God bless you, sir.

Yours sincerely,

Constable D. Butako
Secretary, Korodamu Village Council

On the following afternoon Bulbul brought Ainslie's second reply which Dr Tauvi Mate read out to everyone.

Constable D. Butako
Secretary, Korodamu Village Council

Dear Constable Butako,

God is One, God is Great! Merciful Jesus loves sinners like you
and me. Hallellujah! Thank you for your letter and for the
explicitly detailed medical report, which clearly places your
beloved chairman in the assistable category. I'm happy to inform
you that the High Commission has approved your request. The
New Zealand Government will meet all of Mr Bomboki's
expenses and be responsible for him from his departure until
his return. The High Commission has contacted the Auckland
doctors who will take care of him.

Unfortunately for the moment all the hospitals are fully
occupied and booked, so that Mr Bomboki will not be able to
enter one until fifteen days from today. I have. however, ordered
some pain-killers, which will be flown in tomorrow. Please send
someone to pick them up at my office tomorrow afternoon. They
should give Mr Bomboki relief until he arrives in Auckland.

I would appreciate it if you could arrange to have all his
necessary travel documents ready and bring his passport here
for the visas.

Thank you very much for expressing confidence in us. Yes,
we New Zealanders are as good a people as any on the face of
the earth; and if we have any outstanding virtues, it's because
the Land of the Long White Cloud is God's Own Country, as
everyone but Australians admit. But the Aussies will come to
the party now that we have started walking all over them in test
cricket.

As for your wish to emigrate to Auckland, you are most
welcome to apply although I advise you strongly to do it the
Pacific Way, very slowly. Take your time, we will certainly take
ours. Let things age and mature like the great white wines of
New Zealand. If problems are handled in your justly renowned
Pacific Way, they will eventually and in due course be resolved
to everyone's satisfaction.

If you pray sincerely to Lord Jesus tonight, He will certainly
tell you that Tipota is a most beautiful and wonderful country

to live in, and that there is no need to go anywhere else except for medical treatment.

God bless you.

Yours sincerely,

R. Ainslie

Second Secretary, Immigration

Everyone was happy and relieved, especially Oilei because of the news about the pain-killers. Makarita went to her mother and told her and they cried with relief. Constable Butako went home and wrote his last-ever letter to the New Zealand High Commission.

Mr R. Ainslie
Second Secretary, Immigration
New Zealand High Commission
Paradise Towers, Kuruti

Dear Mr. Ainslie,

God is Great, God is Merciful. Jesus be praised for guiding you to help our beloved chairman, Oilei Bomboki, to go to New Zealand. If you pray to Him again He will tell you that another best and kindest thing to do is to let me go with Oilei to keep him company because he will be very lonely in a strange country. It's part of the Pacific Way that we don't leave sick people alone without the care of those who love them, and Oilei doesn't know anyone in Auckland. When, after the operation, Oilei returns home I'll start my new life in your trouble-free country. I'm very happy to know that New Zealand is called God's Own Country, because it sounds like a Holy Land and I am a very good Christian. I will pay my own fares to Auckland and will stay with my cousin, Tevita Mosi, who will get me a job in the freezing works no problem.

Sir, I put inside this letter two hundred dollars in cash for you to buy something nice for your lovely wife and beer for your kind self. If you want more let me know. After you've read this letter please call me at my office in Korodamu. My telephone number is 696-969. I will come then and get my visas. I want to give up the Pacific Way and do things the New Zealand Way, very fast, just like most of your great white wines, which you age and mature within two days and sell them to us. I love to drink more of the older ones in Auckland.

If you pray to Lord Jesus, He will tell you to stamp a visa for permanent residence in New Zealand on my passport, and when you do that I will give you three hundred dollars more to buy nice things for your beautiful wife.

God bless you.

Yours sincerely,

Constable D. Butako
Secretary, Korodamu Village Council

At eight thirty the following morning Butako went to the New Zealand High Commission, delivered the letter to the receptionist, and caught the bus back to Korodamu, where he waited in his office. The telephone rang at ten thirty.

'Hello there, Mr. Ainslie . . .'

'Is that you, DB? FO here. Listen, mate, you better scram very fast,' said a familiar voice from Police Headquarters.

'What?'

'Scram! Like now! There's a warrant out for your arrest. They're already on the way to haul you in.'

'What for?'

'You fuckwit! You've ballsed it up this time. The Kiwis complained about you trying to bribe one of their officials. You're also wanted for embezzlement. Get lost and don't let them catch you or we'll all end up in gaol. Pick your way carefully to the usual place. We'll get you out. Leave everything. Run!'

A week later, just before a cruise ship the *Orient* disgorged her twelve hundred mostly Australian passengers at the Captain Cook Wharf, half a dozen customs officials boarded her for the usual inspection. One of them, sporting a red handkerchief hanging out of his jacket pocket, picked his way carefully into the lower decks. 'In here!' a voice whispered from one of the cabins. Butako side-stepped inside and closed the door.

'Hand it over now.'

Butako gave the speaker a well-packed envelope.

'Good. I'm Frank Leone, a steward. This is an empty cabin. You stay put inside until we get to Auckland. I'll lock it from outside so that no one else but me can get in or out. There are two chamber-pots under the bunk for your use. I'll clear them every night when I bring your food. There're sandwiches on the top bunk. Also a stack of *Penthouse* and *Hustler* mags. Enjoy them but don't pull yourself too hard or it'll come off. See you later.'

A few days later ex-Constable Butako joined the ranks of tens of thousands of illegal Pacific Island migrants who kept the wheels of New Zealand industries chugging along while the Kiwis were flocking by the tens of thousands to the greener fields of Australia.

Two weeks after he was informed of his assisted treatment in Auckland, a very inebriated Oilei left at dawn on a Pan Pacific Airways flight. As soon as the Boeing 737 was airborne the chief hostess announced that continental breakfast would be served immediately. Having spent all night drinking at a farewell party organised for him, Oilei was quite famished and was looking forward to something filling and delicious. But when his tray was placed before him, his face crumbled.

'Is this entrée?' he blurted out as he looked disgustedly at what was on the tray: one half of a stale croissant and coffee so thin he could see clearly through to the bottom of the cup.

'We don't serve entrée at breakfast, sir,' the hostess answered politely.

'Do you mean that this is all I'm offered?' Oilei demanded crossly. 'No wonder this airline's called Pan Pacific Arsehole!'

'Sir, if you don't like it, I'll take it away,' the hostess suggested calmly.

'Then take the bloody stuff and flush it down the loo. It'll drain easily since it's much smaller than a normal piece of shit!'

Oilei was only briefly upset; he had been in a very good mood for nearly two weeks since the New Zealand High Commission sent him the promised pain-killing tablets. The atmosphere at home had been very good and by the time he left old friends and fellow villagers had been dropping in on him. And just about everyone in Korodamu had gone to the airport to see him off. He thought about all his friends and especially about Makarita and Bulbul, both of whom wept copiously as they bade him farewell.

Halfway to New Zealand Oilei started thinking about Babu and the Mark of the Third Millenium he had stamped on his

141

arse. He was still trying to get Babu off his mind when the captain announced the imminent descent.

From Auckland International Airport Oilei was whisked straight to the Dun Mihaka Memorial Hospital, a ten-storeyed modern building set in spacious surroundings a fair distance from the city centre. He noticed that the place seemed full of sick-looking people. In his single room on the seventh floor he looked out at a small lake, full of ducks and other wading birds. He was amazed at how neat and clean the whole area was. Nothing like what he had seen in Tipota and the neighbouring Island countries.

He opened the window and a rush of cool, crisp air hit his face. Again, it was different from the heavy, muggy atmosphere back home. He supposed that, like the immaculately clean hospital, the outside surroundings were also disinfected. They looked like it from his windows. This is a beautiful, dirt-free country, he told himself. Yet there were so many sickly people around! They could have been foreigners like him, or it could be that clean and ultra-tidy countries have their own kinds of diseases. That was more likely, for many of the diseases in the islands originated from these countries. The pain in the arse could have been one. Damn! He suddenly wished he was at home among the dirt and the muggy air, and especially with Babu, whose disgusting ideas were so disturbingly attractive.

As he was thinking this there was a rattling noise out in the corridor and the door to his room opened. A matronly lady walked in with a tray. It was his lunch. He took one look at the food and said to himself, no wonder they're so sickly; they don't have enough to eat! The amount on the tray was less than a quarter of what he was used to at home. There were some insubstantial green vegetables, carrots and tomatoes but hardly any real food. He became more homesick when he thought of Makarita biting away at two-inch thick slices of bread buttered on both sides. That's a man's food, not this pathetic pile of turd, which Caesar would piss on as soon as he'd seen it. He was contemplating his lunch when a nurse came in.

'You're not eating, are you?'

'I'm not hungry, thank you. I'll wait till dinner.'

'You'd better eat that up, Mr Bomboki. You won't have dinner tonight or breakfast tomorrow. In fact, after that lunch you won't have anything except water until the operation's done.'

'Good God,' Oilei exclaimed and started eating, despite his distaste. He was quite famished and the food made him even hungrier. Another meal like this and I'll be as sick as them, he thought, and became thoroughly depressed.

Later in the afternoon a tired-looking man entered Oilei's room and said in an easy manner, 'Welcome to New Zealand, Mr Bomboki. I hope your flight was pleasant. I'm Albert Fraser, your surgeon for tomorrow's operation. Please tell me as much as you can about your problem, how and when it started, and what was done to it until you came.' Mr Fraser took a chair and sat down, opened a clipboard he had brought and was ready to listen.

It took about two hours for Oilei to give a summary account of his illness and the various treatments he had received, leaving out only the episode with Babu. Mr Fraser was utterly fascinated; he had never before heard anything remotely like it. He listened quietly throughout until Oilei said, 'I didn't try our hospitals because they're dangerous.'

'Dangerous, Mr Bomboki?'

'Yes. Everyone says so. Even Dr Tauvi Mate himself, although he's a senior medical officer in our biggest hospital. People die like flies in those places and most are so afraid of them that they are flocking to our *dottores* like I did.'

'I see,' Mr Fraser quietly dropped the subject. 'Please take your pyjamas off and let me look at the problem.'

He opened Oilei's buttocks, closed them quickly and rushed out of the room. When he returned, his face was behind a scented mask and his hands in elbow-length transparent gloves. He examined Oilei's bottom once again, thoroughly this time, shoving in an instrument like those used by doctors to examine people's ears. Then he left the room, telling Oilei to get dressed and wait. In a little while he returned, sat down and looked at his patient for a long time before speaking.

'If I had not examined your anus, I would not have believed half the things you told me. My God, why did you let those quacks do what they did to your bottom?'

'I had no choice. I was desperate.'

'I see. But they have certainly left their marks all over your arse, er, anus. You not only have fistulae, your anus looks as if someone had taken to it with a digging fork. Christ, it'll be a difficult one to operate on, I can tell you that.'

'What are you going to do about it then, doctor?'

'We'll see tomorrow after we've scanned it thoroughly. In the meantime have a good rest. You'll need all you can get.'

Oilei was all the more depressed that evening when he thought of Makarita gorging herself on taro and tinned fish.

When he woke the following morning he was not even allowed to drink anything. At about nine a nurse entered with a tray. Oilei smiled and sat up quickly and hopefully. But when he saw what was on the tray his spirits sank. There was a pair of scissors, a razor, some powder, a syringe and a small bottle of clear liquid.

'Good morning. Ready for the shave?'

'That's OK. I'll do it myself, thank you,' he said, reaching out for the razor.

The nurse restrained him. 'You just lie down, Mr Bomboki. I'll shave you down there.'

'Where?'

'There and there,' she replied, indicating Oilei's front and back sides.

'Oh, shit! Sorry. Why?'

'Preparation for surgery, Mr Bomboki. We do it when people are operated on down there.'

'Couldn't you get a man to do it?'

'Don't let me upset you. I've done it to hundreds of men. Means nothing really; I'm used to it.'

'But I'm not,' Oilei protested.

'We don't have much time, Mr Bomboki. Please lie down and relax.'

'How could you expect me to relax under the circumstances?'

But he took off his pyjamas, stretched out and closed his eyes. He felt the nurse's hands at work, manhandling his totally flaccid organs, pushing or pulling them out of the way for the scissors and the razor. When she had finished she pushed and pulled things around some more as she made sure that every hair had been removed. Oilei was by then peering through his left eye at her. Then he peered at himself and at once understood what Samson must have felt after he had been shorn by his very own Delilah.

'Please turn on your stomach. I'll shave your bottom.'

'Shit on your face!' Oilei blurted out in Tipotan and turned over roughly.

'Beg your pardon?'

'Oh. I said, "Yes, Sister."'

'Yeah, it sounded like it too,' she rejoined lightly and carried on.

'That's all thank you. Now, let's see your arm.' She prepared the syringe and injected him. 'You've just been sedated. Soon you'll feel relaxed and a bit dopey. Then they'll come and get you.'

A great calm settled on Oilei. Things looked and sounded as if they were at a great distance. He felt completely detached from everything, including himself. Two men wheeled in a trolley and helped him onto it. He felt every turn of the wheels as they propelled him along corridors, in and out of a lift and, after what seemed like an interminably long time, they entered a theatre or what looked more like a lecture auditorium filled with scores of young men and women. Perhaps the whole School of Medicine of the Auckland University was there to witness the performance and to wonder at his arse? Mr Fraser had assured him that it would be a difficult operation. Oilei registered these thoughts without engaging his emotions. Then the surgeon's tired but smiling face loomed over him. 'Good morning. We'll put you to sleep now,' he heard the voice say and felt a hand on his shoulder. A needle pricked his arm and he drifted into blackness.

Using special equipment, including an anus scanner, Mr Fraser saw and identified all that was wrong with Oilei's bottom. He turned to the student audience.

'There are twenty-two fistulae in the patient's anus, which is almost certainly the largest number ever found in a single such orifice at any one time. The whole complex is shockingly lacerated and ulcerous owing to rough treatment he got at home. This anus is absolutely beyond repair. I will have to lift out the entire organ and replace it with another. It's the only way to save this poor, wretched creature.' So saying, he turned to a nurse standing behind.

'Sister Agnes, please go to the Spare Parts Chamber and fetch an appropriate anus.'

He wrote on a piece of paper the exact specifications of what was needed. While the sister was away, the surgeon deftly and delicately carved out Oilei's diseased arse and threw it into a large bin.

Sister Agnes returned with a bottle filled with clear fluid in which a spare anus was throbbing and swimming like a jelly-fish. Mr Fraser examined it thoroughly, his face turning redder all the while.

'This is a white woman's anus, Sister Agnes. I clearly specified a male Polynesian organ! Go back there and get the right one, hop to it!'

'I'm sorry, Mr Fraser, there aren't any Polynesian arseholes in the chamber.'

'What? Why, Sister Agnes?'

'Those coconuts don't donate their backsides to medical science. The one or two we ever got were rejected outright on account of the state they were in.'

'Shit! Go back there and get a male organ, Sister Agnes. This feminist arsehole will never do!'

'Why?'

'She doesn't like men, that's why.'

'Are you all right, Mr Fraser?'

'Of course I'm not all right! How could I be with this crazy arsehole poking her tongue at me? Look at her!'

'I'm afraid that you may have to make do with her . . . it, I mean, Mr Fraser. It's the only one that comes anywhere close to what what you specified.'

'Shit oh shit!' the surgeon exclaimed. After he had regained a measure of sanity, he said resignedly, 'Well, I suppose we'll have to make do with what we've got, won't we? But it's utterly crazy. Fancy a black man walking around with a white feminist arsehole, Jeeesus!'

'It doesn't matter, sir, no one'll see her!' a medical student called out as the whole theatre erupted.

'Don't bet your arse on it, mate,' Mr Fraser retorted and proceeded to insert the spare part into the patient's bottom. He was just about to stitch it on when Oilei's backside rose precipitously and exploded a mighty fart, ejecting the strange anus so fast up into the ceiling that Fraser did not see what had happened. But Sister Agnes, fully alert, dived low across the room, caught the falling organ centimetres from the floor, rose, walked back and handed it over nonchalantly to the thoroughly befuddled surgeon.

'Let's try again,' Mr Fraser said after he had collected his senses. He re-inserted the organ, but as before Oilei shot it out even more violently. This time Sister Agnes, who was crouching like a test cricket wicketkeeper, caught it expertly before it had travelled a metre.

'It's a clear indication that the patient's body will not accept this foreign organ, Mr Fraser,' she said quietly.

'Then get his real thing out and we'll sew it back on.'

It took Sister Agnes ten minutes to locate Oilei's discarded anus from among the bits and pieces of human anatomy in the bin.

'You can't use it, Mr Fraser. This arsehole's as dead as a piece of shit!'

'Jesus Christ. That's all we need to finish him off. He's a dead man, poor bastard. O Lord, why did I agree to operate on him?'

'There's still hope, Mr Fraser,' Sister Agnes suggested. 'Let's send him with the live spare part to the special clinic. They may be able to fix it. They're a peculiar lot but have been successful with virtually every case we've sent them, even after we'd given up all hope.'

'You handle it then, Sister. I'm going home. I promise you I will never again touch another arsehole except my own.'

As soon as he had left and the theatre was cleared of medical students, two men wheeled Oilei out and into a lift that took them down to the basement. They propelled him along a maze of corridors until at last they arrived at a door above which was a sign printed in large letters 'The Whakapohane Clinic'.

Oilei thought that he heard Mr Fraser's voice calling him from a great distance when he was just waking up. He opened his eyes and saw a remarkable and familiar face smiling down at him. He turned his head slowly to one side and then another and registered other familiar faces in a large room with only a few pieces of furniture. Since he could not believe what he had seen he thought that he was hallucinating on account of his sedation. He closed his eyes and when he reopened them the same remarkable image was smiling down at him. With much effort he lifted his hand and touched the face.

'Is it really you?'

'Yes, it's me indeed,' Babu Vivekanand replied.

'How could it be?'

'All in due course, Brother Oilei. You've been under my care for the past six weeks. You're recovering strongly.'

'I'm sorry, but I don't feel strong. I think that I'm slipping away.'

'You're feeling weak partly because of what those butchers up there did to you. And you've been unconscious for most of the past six weeks. But your body is strong and mending quickly. Look around you, I had them brought here five weeks ago to help bring you back from the brink of death.'

Oilei looked around again and there was no doubt about it; they were there: Makarita, Bulbul Bohut, Losana Tonoka, a newly slim Marama Kakase, Domoni Thimailomalangi, Seru Draunikau, Dr James Hamilton, Dr Sigmund Zimmerman, and most surprising of all, Dr Kati Kanikani, the Tipotan Minister for Health. Standing behind them was ex-constable Dau Butako, who, as it turned out, was rescued by Babu from the gutters of Ponsonby and transformed into a Millenarian. There were also an American and an Eastern European who were introduced to Oilei as Babu's good friends.

'Rita,' Oilei called out softly.

Makarita moved up, kissed him lightly and whispered, 'I love you, my sweet spouse.'

'You have joined.'

'Yes. And I've been branded with the Mark of the Third Millenium,' Makarita said proudly and sat down on the chair beside the bed. She held his hands as he closed his eyes and drifted away with his lips frozen in an act of kissing something. Something wonderful, Makarita thought.

A week later Oilei woke up from his long sleep to the sound of people chanting a monotonous tune with only two words repeated over and over in various combinations: *holy holy/ holy yoga/ yoga holy/ yoga yoga*, and so on. Slowly he became aware of lying on his stomach, his lower half off the end of the bed, feet wide apart and planted on the floor. He felt much stronger and his head was clear.

He looked around and saw everyone he had seen when he woke up last, not knowing when that was. Everyone except Bulbul, Makarita and Constable Butako was singing and dancing in a circle around the bed. Losana was at the head with Babu bringing up the rear. They were all stark naked. The other three, the new recruits, were in a far corner of the room practising first-stage yoga.

As Oilei made to shift position, Babu called out, 'Don't move, please. We're just beginning your final treatment. We will bestow on you the collective kiss of love and respect, the best treatment there is for every disease and sickness known to humankind. Please remain as you are until the treatment's completed. We will leave this hospital as soon as it's over.'

Oilei kept still while the music picked up tempo and strength; the singers danced faster and faster, kicking, rolling, grinding and pirouetting, demonstrating some of the most strikingly beautiful combinations of classical ballet and breakdance movements he had seen. Suddenly the music stopped and the dancers fell into a line behind Oilei with Losana Tonoka still in front and Babu at the back.

'Bend forward,' Babu said quietly and everyone obeyed, their noses stopping a centimetre off the bottoms of the persons in front. Oilei could feel the heat of Losana's face brushing his derrière.

'Breathe in . . . Breathe out . . . Nose in place . . .' Noses went

149

into place and Oilei felt Losana's great hooked snout enter his extreme aperture.

'Breathe in . . . Breathe out . . . Breathe in . . . Breathe out . . .' Babu commanded rhythmically for a few minutes before he implanted his nose into Dr Zimmerman's anus and called out, 'For the last time . . . Breathe in . . . Breathe out . . . Disengage nose . . . Sing!' And they all sang the great hymn of the Third Millenium into each other's Eternity.

Oilei basked in the indescribable sensation that enveloped his whole being and transported him into the throbbing core of the Anus of the Universe, the Soul Essence of the One Infinite. He was at peace with himself and at one with the Onmipresent Nothingness. All that had troubled him had evaporated. It had happened much sooner than it should but the emergency had compelled Babu to carry him over before he had travelled the required steps. He would do this later.

They filed quietly out of the Whakapohane Clinic, out of the Dun Mihaka Memorial Hospital and into the Mt Eden mansion of a professor at the University of Auckland to wait for their flights to their various destinations. The professor was an extraordinary man: he stood 130 centimetres tall and was reputedly the smallest academic in the whole southern hemisphere.

'He looks like an elf, so tiny and mischievous,' Oilei remarked as soon as he saw him.

'Don't be deceived by appearances, Brother Oilei,' Babu admonished. 'Our beloved host and fellow Millenarian may be wanting in height, but his anus is as wide as the Portals of Paradise.'

In the next few days Oilei arranged and rearranged fragments of information he had gleaned, until a clear picture emerged. For many years Babu had worked clandestinely in Asia, America and Europe, developing and propagating his unique philosophy for peace. Fabulously generous donations from people and organisations had enabled him to establish the Third Millenium Foundation (TMF) for the purpose of sponsoring, among other things, grand international conferences that gave him the opportunity to spread his message widely.

When it became clear that the centre for world civilisation

would soon shift to the Pacific, Babu and his followers moved to Nanggaralevu in anticipation. As part of its Pacific operation, the TMF funded the memorable International Conference on the Promotion of Understanding and Co-operation between Traditional and Modern Sciences of Medicine held in the Tipotan capital. With a contingent of his most able disciples, Babu attended the conference and worked on the participants. All the twelve hundred of them who went to the opening of the International School of Traditional Medicine (ISTM) were duly converted to his movement.

After his rescue from St Martins Mental Hospital, Babu returned to his base in Fiji and then travelled on to other Island countries, before heading to New Zealand to accept on behalf of the ISTM the gift of the Whakapohane Clinic from the board of governors of the Dun Mihaka Memorial Hospital. He had spent about a month in the clinic, doing great deeds. He was just about to leave for Australia, where enthusiastic workers were already operating out of the Wayward Chapel in King's Cross, Sydney, when Oilei was wheeled in.

Babu had managed to insert the spare anus into Oilei's bottom but in order to prevent its rejection he had to leave his nose in there for almost twenty-four hours a day. His mastery of yoga enabled him to remain inside Oilei's fundament for prolonged periods, but, realising that he could not go on with it indefinitely, he contacted the CIA in Wellington to bring the others in from Nanggaralevu. They all took turns over the weeks, and twice every day performed the song and dance ritual.

Makarita was flown to Auckland to keep Oilei quiet because during his long sleep he screamed many times for his wife, exerting dangerous pressure on his new anus. Bulbul went off on his own volition; when he heard that Makarita had left he suspected that Oilei was dying.

'But how did you get yourself a clinic in a modern hospital?' Oilei asked.

'Simple, really. You see, because of the recommendations of the great conference in Tipota, an increasing number of hospitals throughout the world now provide facilities for the practice of traditional medicine. The collaboration between the old and new

151

sciences of medicine is fast becoming a matter of course.'

'You've established an institution for the recruitment of *dottores* and have won many of them over. But what about the doctors?'

That's the next stage of our development plan,' Babu looked very holy. 'We've already negotiated with the appropriate authorities for the establishment of the first International School of New Modern Medicine as a faculty of the University of the Southern Paradise. Once that is set up, hopefully within the next twelve months, we'll get most of the doctors in the Pacific Rim and Basin. Dr Hamilton will be the first Head of the School, with Dr Zimmerman as his deputy. Both are dedicated Millenarians.

'At the University we have only just converted three top professors and the head of socio . . . er, I mean head of a particular department. They are marvellous and enthusiastic Millenarians, toiling selflessly for the great cause and promising to deliver the entire academic staff within two years. They're far more effective than any missionary in the history of humankind.

'Our CIA friends are also working on the vice-chancellor, the registrar, the bursar, heads of departments, schools, institutes and extension studies. It's only a matter of time, given the rising amount of aid funds CIA's dishing out, before they too become Millenarians. I'm afraid, however, that the great organs of these eminent personalities need quite a lot of scrubbing and smoothing. But we've sent orders to our factories in Tokyo and Hong Kong for supplies of very special antibiotic detergent, steel brushes and antiseptic sandpaper for the purpose. No problem there, really.'

On the flight back home Oilei sat on a window seat next to Makarita. He looked out at the cloudless sky, thinking about all that he had undergone. His agony was only a blurred memory. He could hardly imagine how it had felt without actually feeling it again.

His arse had been preached at, prayed upon, exorcised, breathed into and out of, sung and danced. It had been exploded, jabbed, blown, hummed, needled, steamed, smoked, carved, discarded, transplanted, race-transformed, sex-changed, nosed and kissed back to life. No human arse had been subjected to so many trials and tribulations. No human orifice had gone through hell to emerge in the end so strong, so healthy and so wise. He and his lowliest organ had been called upon to the great task of saving humanity from its headlong rush toward the Apocalypse, and ushering in a new millenium of lasting peace, prosperity and happiness. He remembered Bulbul's prophetic words: 'Marxism and Communism have shaken the twentieth century; the Pan Pacific Philosophy for Peace and the Third Millenium will shake the twenty-first and beyond.'

Kiss my arse!